The Unicorn Clan

The Unicorn are unlike any other samurai clan, for despite the insular and xenophobic society of Rokugan, the Clan of Shinjo spent most of its history beyond the borders of the Emerald Empire. Known as the Ki-Rin Clan in the early days of the Empire, following the Day of Thunder, Shinjo led her followers on a journey to seek out new threats outside of Rokugan and deal with them before they might bring war or calamity to the Empire. When it returned almost eight centuries later, the clan now calling itself Unicorn was almost unrecognizable to the other Great Clans.

The Shinjo family bears the name of the clan's founding Kami, and its daimyō holds the title "Khan of Khans." The Shinjo are great war-leaders and diplomats both. Serving the spiritual needs of the clan, the Iuchi family achieves miraculous effects through a strange practice they call meishōdō, developed in the absence of Rokugan's kami. The Utaku family is known for its battle maidens, an elite order of warriors known for their devotion to Bushidō and their majestic steeds, both unparalleled in Rokugan. The insightful and charismatic Ide are the ambassadors and traders of the clan, both within Rokugan and along the Sand Road. Uniquely within Rokugan, the Moto family descends from a people encountered beyond its borders, the Ujik. A family of these steppe nomads swore their service to Shinjo herself, and so none can gainsay their status as Rokugani, despite their unusual ways.

The Unicorn Clan continues its duty to safeguard Rokugan from external threats, but also continues to bring new goods, arts, and ideas into the Empire. It maintains the border city of Khanbulak, one end of the great trade route known as the Sand Road, which the clan administers. In this way, even as the other Great Clans continue to deride the Unicorn for their strange practices, their unique situation brings them wealth and influence.

A
Legend of the Five Rings™
novella

Across the Burning Sands

By Daniel Lovat Clark

Fantasy Flight Games

Chapter One: The Way Station

I rode past two white trees.

It grew so dark I could hardly see.

Tried to go home, but never again.

I'd ridden clean out of the realms of men.

The attackers were poised to kill them all in three ways. The first was the spear and bow, the spilling of blood: the honorable path, in other words. The killers, who wore furs and leathers and stank of animal fat, carried torches, axes, spears, and crude bows. Although Shono and his party were samurai and the brigands were only Tegensai mountain folk come down from the Pillar of the Sky, only a fool would think that death did not rest at the ends of those weapons.

I am no fool. I have seen death come too suddenly, too soon. He remembered another battle, the feel of his sword in his hand as it bit flesh.

The second way was via the animals: horses and camels, but mainly horses. One hundred of the beasts were kept in the paddocks of the way station. If the ambushers could kill or steal those beasts, Shono and his samurai would never reach the next way station alive.

Tegensai have little use for our horses in their mountains, except perhaps to feed them to their dogs and the mountain trolls. But it didn't matter why they might want the mounts—only that Shono's party would die on foot.

The third was water. Always water—on the Sand Road, even there on the knees of the Pillar of the Sky mountains. A heavy stone cistern lay on the rise above the way station. The lid must have weighed as much as thirty warriors, but it could be moved or broken. If the water were poisoned or befouled or spilled into the thirsty dust of the Sand Road, they would sicken and die, humans and horses both.

Shono's life was an inch from ending in three different ways, but what of it? *Does a samurai not live at all times three feet from death?* He walked from the yurt with no sign of fear. *Mitsuko is dead. I was to make her my wife, and instead I made her a corpse. What have I left to lose?*

Shono drove a handful of arrows into the dust at his feet, seeing his mother's grave face as she sent him west. *"To treat with the caliph in al-Zawira."* As if the entire clan couldn't see it for what it was: sending her broken son away. He drew, loosed—as calm, as numb, as in the practice yard. His arrow struck true, and a man died. *What of it?*

"Lord Shono!" Three of his retinue, weapons in hand, surrounded him. Yumino was wearing her armor—*Does she sleep in it?*—but the Bokudō brothers were like him, protected only by an Ujik-style *deel* of dyed wool. "Lord Shono," said Yumino again. "We should get you away from here."

"No," he said. His voice, his orders, but Shono watched, heard them happen, as if he were someone else watching another person standing in his skin. He commanded only by force of habit. "Yumino-san, to the cistern. Naosuke-san, Naotaka-san, see to the horses."

"That's right, send the shepherd to tend the horses," quipped Taka.

"Plenty of goats between us and them," added his brother. But they went; of course they did. Only city people would mistake the nomads' free spirit for a lack of discipline. Shono knew better.

So Shono stood alone again, plucking a harvest of death from the sandy soil at his feet and sending it streaking into the chaos and dark. Each shot stung at his wrist where his bracer should have been—he almost felt it. Most of his arrows found their mark, sending Tegensai warriors sprawling. Others vanished into the dark. Shono saw no difference between the two from his place outside his own mind, watching himself at work.

Soon the arrows were spent. *What of it?* He cast his bow aside and drew his sword. Two of the raiders rushed toward him, one armed with a spear, the other with an axe in her hand. Shono flowed like water, the way his instructors had taught him, wondering if he was about to die even as he knocked the spear aside and stepped inside its reach. The thought did not frighten him.

His sword flashed in the flickering light of the torches and the raiders' spreading fire, intercepting the second brigand's arcing axe blow at the wrist. Axe and hand tumbled into the night. Shono never stopped moving, driving his hip into the spear-wielding brigand and sending him stumbling back. The man shouted something in the language of the Tegensai, and Shono's sword finished its long arc, up and around and back across the raider's chest. It wasn't a fatal wound—the layers of leather and fur cut before his skin—but it was enough to cause him to drop his spear and drive both hands to his breast to stop the blood flow. No samurai, this raider—and young, inexperienced. Shono killed him in another heartbeat. Drove his sword into the man's stomach, watched him fall, gasping for breath.

Just like Mitsuko. For a moment it was her gasping at his feet, the wind snatching her last words from him. It was her blood on his sword. Mitsuko, his betrothed, the hope for peace between Unicorn and Lion. *Dead by my hand, killed as much by my mother's choice as my blade.*

Footsteps behind him. He turned, too slow, still seeing Mitsuko—would he see her again, now? Was this it? A Tegensai raider screamed forward, hurling her spear. It was true, the sweet frisson of perfection that he had felt so many times when an arrow left his bow. It would take him in the heart. He was neither surprised nor afraid. *So I end. What of it?*

But then Taka was there, Bokudō Naotaka, the shepherd's son from the north. According to Rokugani custom, he was *jizamurai,* a vassal warrior not truly noble, not truly peasant. But in the free-spirited Unicorn Clan, a man like Taka could rise to a great station based on his deeds and his skill—deeds like saving Shono's life. The spear took Taka, instead, as he hurled Shono to the ground.

"'See to the horses,'" Taka groaned. "Shono, you ass. As if we would let you fight alone." Then he lay still.

The Tegensai raider lay dead on the ground, Taka's own spear protruding from her chest like a slender tree. Taka's eyes stared at nothing, his face ashen grey.

Mitsuko dead by my hand. Taka dead by my incompetence.

Shono shook his head, scattering windblown dust from his face. *Suke.* He found the other Bokudō brother at the horse paddock, scimitar flashing as he drove a raider back. *Yumino.* She was atop the cistern, her spear flicking forward and back like a lunging serpent. *The others.* Ide Ryōma—language tutor, advisor, friend— hurled a bucketful of water at a burning yurt. Iuchi Shoan—who'd saved his life as a child and been his auntie ever since—tended to a wounded warrior in the doorway of the stone block house of the way station. Other samurai and *ashigaru* lay dead or fought the raiders. His party had numbered twenty warriors when they left Khanbulak. How many raiders were there? Fifty? How many of his own were still alive? A dozen?

They're all going to die. They followed me, and I'm going to get them killed.

He spared a moment to shut Taka's eyes, then started moving. There was no thought, no genius moment of strategy, only the knowledge that to do nothing was to watch a dozen more Takas die in front of his eyes. He rushed to the paddock, took another bandit from behind, and vaulted the fence. "Suke-san, open the gate," Shono said, finding Umeboshi and leaping atop the blood bay's back. No saddle, no stirrup; only a fool or the best rider in the world would fight like this from horseback.

Suke opened the gate, and Shono rode out with a shout. He gripped Boshi's flanks with his knees, one hand tangled in the horse's dark mane; it was barely enough to keep him ahorse. Umeboshi was half in a panic, the smell of blood and fire and the stinking Tegensai all in his nostrils, and eager to rush forward. Shono urged him toward the closest knot of raiders, where two of his retinue were pressed back to back. He slashed at the closest raider as they thundered past, a weak strike given his lack of footing but enough to disrupt their formation, send them scrambling. His warriors took advantage of the distraction and retreated, regrouping at the way station.

Shono kept riding, scattering Tegensai warriors as he ran,

ducking under a hurled spear here, a flickering arrow there. Umeboshi screamed as Shono wrenched him back to the fray time and again. Boshi lashed out with his hooves, shattering bones, screaming and biting. Then one of the Tegensai raiders plunged a spear into Umeboshi's side, and he fell. Shono barely tumbled free in time, failed to keep a hand on his sword.

Not Boshi, too, Shono thought. A ridiculous concern—what did a horse matter compared to the human lives dying around him? *Compared to Mitsuko.*

But the raiders ignored the horse, leapt over him and around him as Boshi struggled to rise again. Two of them: one holding a spear, the other drawing a glimmering long knife. Shinseist prayer beads dangled from the wrist holding the knife. *The Lion reject Shinsei, the Tegensai accept him, and both try to kill me.* Shono reached to his hip and drew his *wakizashi*. He backed away, turning his head and letting his senses drift across the battlefield in the Shinjo fashion, searching for a path to safety. He heard hoofbeats.

"Now you die, *chi-gye*," the spearman growled in broken Rokugani. Then the point of a lance burst from his breast, and he fell as a frothing horse galloped past. The bandit with the knife had enough time to turn before a scimitar flashed in the dark and his head fell from his shoulders. A great black horse reared, bellowing, in front of Shono, its rider booming in the dark.

"Cousin!" Chagatai called. "It seems the Moto come to the aid of the Shinjo once again!"

2. The Sand Road

Behold the setting sun; it leaves a trail of gold.

Someday I will follow it as Shinjo did in days of old.

To ride into the Burning Sands where the nights are icy cold,

That is my destiny, for only Ki-Rin could be so bold.

They left the way station the next day, descending from the Pillar of the Sky mountains and riding into the endless sweep of the Plain of Wind and Stone. Red hills lay like a crumpled blanket before them, edging on a rolling expanse of black-and-yellow earth. Ribbons of sand lay against spurs of rock, and flats of dusty clay were interrupted by ragged scars left by the infrequent rivers of the Burning Sands. A few clumps of blue-green marked where hardy shrubs clung to what life they could eke out of the land. *Beautiful and empty. I could ride into that expanse and be gone forever.*

Chagatai's warriors added to Shono's party made their group almost forty strong, with over a hundred horses. Shono, Chagatai, Yumino, and Ide Ryōma rode apart from the main body, where the thunder of hooves and dust of the trail was less oppressive.

The conversation, however, is stifling.

Moto Chagatai kept up a steady flow of boasts and chatter throughout the morning. He praised Shono's horse—the blue roan Tsubasa that day, while Umeboshi recuperated—and pronounced the virtues of his own, a black stallion named Daichin.

"Your horse is very fine, Cousin," said Shono.

Chagatai proclaimed his love of hunting, asking his cousin if he fancied their chances of finding any worthy game on their ride today.

"I have never been so far west," said Shono. "I must bow to your superior expertise in this matter, Chagatai-san."

A mistake. The man will pounce on my weakness.

"So you must, Shono-kun," agreed Chagatai. "It is a wise lord who knows when to accept the wisdom of his betters."

"And a wise officer who can offer his expertise when it is warranted, yet hold his tongue when his silence is preferred," observed Ryōma. The little man's round hat was pulled down against the sun, and his lazy way of slouching atop his horse gave the impression that he was asleep. "We were speaking of hunting. In your opinion, Chagatai-sama, are we likely to find any worthwhile game on our journey today?"

"How can we speak of hunting, with our friends' ashes still warm?" asked Yumino.

"Dead is dead," said Chagatai. "The rites have been said and the Lords of Death appeased, and the ashes ride east with my messengers to be returned to their families. Meanwhile, we living must ride on."

"And we must eat," said Ryōma.

"Yes," agreed Chagatai. "As for game, we may see a deer or two when next we find water, but I fear they will have fled the sound of our hooves. I did see two fine birds in your baggage, Cousin; perhaps falconry can fetch a hare or two between us."

"Those birds are intended as gifts for the caliph," said Ryōma.

"Some exercise may do them good," Shono allowed. He turned Tsubasa back to the main column.

In so doing, he bought himself a frigid reception from Suke, who found an excuse to ride to the far end of their party. *I earned that.* But if Suke's mood persisted, or spread, it could make his warriors unruly, erode their discipline. *I cannot lead them if they do not trust me. They will not trust me if I do not trust myself.* Watching himself from the outside, he saw what he should do, the overtures he should make, the balance of command and friendship. But it was impossible. There was nothing inside him to make the connection with. *Perhaps I should step aside. Retreat to a monastery; would that make things right?*

He accepted the birds from his groom, Tanaka, and rode back to Chagatai. Suke's mood would have to wait. *As will my own.*

They distributed the hawks and rode out farther from the main column, sending the birds aloft when a rabbit burst from a scrap of scraggly bush. Chagatai's bird made the kill, and he rode off to collect it with a chuckle.

"Shono-sama." *She doesn't even touch the reins.* Yumino nudged her sacred steed over to where Shono sat on Tsubasa. "I worry that Chagatai is trying to get you away from the protection of the column."

"Ah," murmured Ryōma from Shono's other side. "You, too, are wondering at the coincidence that those bandits just happened to attack a way station for the first time in years as the Shinjo heir was passing through."

Chagatai, trying to kill me? The thought neither surprised him nor frightened him. *Would that balance the scales?* "You forget, it was Chagatai who rode to our rescue. Without his intervention, I would be dead. So might we all be."

Yumino grunted and turned away, her horse moving instantly from a standstill to a gallop.

"She thinks that she's failed you as a *yōjimbō*," Ryōma said. "Take care not to sting her pride any more than is necessary, Shono-sama. The Battle Maidens swear no oaths, waste no words on empty promises. That she has chosen to serve you is a mark of high honor."

"Yumino-san did her duty, and I am still alive," Shono said. "What more could either of us ask for?"

"As you say," said Ryōma in that tone that meant the opposite. He quieted again and appeared to fall asleep in his saddle.

When Chagatai returned, he had a fine dust-brown rabbit hanging from his saddle, and the caliph's bird perched proudly on his gauntlet. "Your hawk is still aloft, Shono-san," he called. "Does the bird refuse your commands?"

"She cannot refuse commands I have not issued," said Shono.

"A curious sentiment—one who never gives an order is never refused. Tell me, is this how you intend to rule, when you become khan?" Chagatai sidled Daichin into step as Shono urged Tsubasa forward. Ryōma and Yumino fell in behind.

"The Emperor rules," said Shono. "The khan leads."

"Have you a different opinion, Chagatai-sama?" asked Ryōma. "Your own father is the Moto khan; has he taught you the difference between a ruler and a leader?"

"Let the Ide shave words apart for their meanings," said Chagatai. "We Moto prefer actions to words. My father, Ögodei Khan, rules the western lands well and leads our armies when he must. When I am khan, I will do both with brilliance."

"Khan of the Moto," asked Yumino, "or Khan of Khans? You forget your station, Chagatai-sama."

"*Che,*" breathed Chagatai, shaking his head. "And why not? I have the Kami's blood in my veins, the same as my cousin here. Where is it written that the Khan of Khans must always be a Shinjo?" He held the rabbit aloft. "I can hunt, I can ride, and no one alive is as deadly on horseback as I; the Unicorn would be lucky to have a khan such as me." He glanced sidelong at Shono. "Especially in a time of war, *ne?*"

A war I gave us, with Mitsuko's blood on my sword.

"You do not choose the khan," growled Yumino.

"Ha! No, I don't. But perhaps someone should. A *quriltai*, as in days of old. Let the Unicorn choose who will lead them."

For a moment, Shono wanted it. *If I step aside, let Chagatai be khan, I could—what? Will it bring her back? Will I forsake my duty?* Bushidō forbade such thinking. He hoped that keen pulse of longing hadn't shown on his face.

"I could kill you where you stand for such disloyalty," hissed Yumino.

"You could try," laughed Chagatai. "But be at ease, Yumino-san. Shono is in no danger from me. That is what you fear, is it not?" Rolling with his horse's gait, Chagatai carefully hooded his hawk, placing her on the horn of his saddle. "You wonder at the bandit attack, at my convenient arrival. Well, it was no accident. I rode west when I received word from my aunt, Moto Rurame Noyan, about a spy captured in Khanbulak." He turned in his saddle and smiled, broad and smug like a hunting cat. "If I ever wish you dead, Cousin, I'll do the job myself. I won't be sending brigands to accost you on the road."

"It's likely someone did, though," Ryōma mused. "An enemy without Chagatai-sama's refreshing forthrightness."

Shono raised his hand, and his hawk fell from the sky with a shriek to perch atop his leather gauntlet. "There is no sport to be had here," he said, "and the column is drawing ahead of us." He put his heels to Tsubasa's flank, and they broke into a gallop.

Two days later, they reached the Hidden Valley, where the Ganzu family made their home. The journey was uneventful, aside from a spirited chase after a wounded antelope that put Chagatai, pink faced with the thrill of the hunt, in a gregarious mood for more than a day.

Shono spent the journey studying his cousin, his thundering moods. Chagatai was as wild as the desert through which they rode, as sudden as a grasslands storm, a Moto to the bone. Shono tried to imagine him at a formal court occasion, sitting meekly through a tea ceremony or—Fortunes, kami, and Lords of Death forbid—in audience with the Emperor himself. *A wild stallion loosed in a porcelain maker's workshop. There would be no survivors.* Chagatai was everything the Empire thought of the Unicorn: wild, free, fierce, quick to laugh, quick—according to himself—to love, terrible to anger, generous, and almost completely lacking in social graces. Yet he was beloved by his fellow Unicorn. When one of the ashigaru started up the traveling song, Chagatai joined in enthusiastically. His verses celebrated the legendary Moto skill in battle while also alluding to their great prowess as lovers. Shono himself couldn't find the music within him. *Perhaps my mother would approve of Chagatai. Didn't she break off her engagement to Ikoma Anakazu, knowing it might mean war with the Lion Clan, out of fear the Unicorn might cease to be ourselves? When we put on the silk robes of court, climb down from our horses, and bow to the other clans, do we abandon what makes us who we are? Would a khan like Chagatai earn us the respect we have been denied?*

He had no answers. He wished to share his thoughts with Ide Ryōma, explain how his murder of his betrothed had tainted him, how stepping aside for Chagatai could make things right. Except if he did that, if he admitted to the weakness of his thoughts, he would lose the respect of Ryōma and everyone who served him. *This is not Bushidō.* Instead, he tried to imagine what the little Ide would say: "*It is also the Unicorn way to adapt, to new environments or to new people. We adapted when we stayed with the Ujik and adopted the Moto into our clan. We must adapt again now that we are returned to Rokugan.*" Chagatai could never change who he was. Shono could never ask him to, no more than put the wild hawk on the wing in a cage. *Something beautiful would be lost forever. Is that the burden of the Khan of Khans, to put themself in the cage and keep their clan free?* And was his mother's choice sacrificing her own honor to preserve Unicorn freedom, or was it sacrificing the honor of her clan to break herself out of the cage? *Will we ever agree on an answer to that one?*

Shono's musings were brushed aside as the Hidden Valley appeared before him. He'd had no warning as they approached it. In all directions, he'd seen nothing but the desolation of the Burning Sands. The Pillar of the Sky mountains were a gentle bruise in the sky behind them, and the sweep of rock and sand extended like an ocean all around. Then, suddenly, they were atop a rise looking down into a broad river valley, green with water and filled with box-shaped mounds of baked earth. Roadways of weathered wood bridged mound to mound, and people in striped robes with turbans wrapped around their heads made their way throughout what must have been a city, only Shono could see no buildings. One man arrived at a mound like any other, took leave of his companion, and then descended a stair into the earth.

"Welcome to the Hidden Valley," laughed Chagatai. "It makes an impression, does it not?"

"They live beneath the earth," Shono said at length.

"Indeed they do," said Chagatai. "As you might, in this sun-scorched land. And it has the advantage that, as no rooftops or towers rise above the fall of the river valley, the whole village is invisible from more than a dozen yards away."

"Can these people truly be Rokugani?" breathed Yumino in wonder.

"Some in the Imperial Court might say the same of the Ujik," said Ryōma. "But in point of law, no; the Ganzu are Unicorn by our custom, but not of Rokugan. Our holdings beyond the Emperor's proclaimed borders are…a special case."

"The Emperor cares not whether his subjects live above or below the ground," declared Chagatai, "so long as they pay their taxes."

"And we care not," said Shono, "so long as they have water."

Chagatai's eyes were upon him as they gathered at the head of the switchback trail on the valley slopes that led to a broad paddock at the downstream edge of the village. *Is even this a test? Does Chagatai see some weakness, some failing in how I respond to the Ganzu?* He couldn't fathom the *noyan*'s game. He couldn't fathom his own response to it. So he ignored it, as best he could.

This eastern bank was given over mainly to the strange sunken city, its narrow courtyards and orchards recessed between raised earthen walls and roads. The western bank was entirely agricultural, with fruit-laden trees in uneven rows and squares of black earth bearing a crop of some sort of grain, its stalks nearly doubled over with the weight of their seed. Seeing so much lush greenery after weeks of some of the least hospitable landscape he'd ever encountered was a surprise that left Shono feeling untethered, adrift in memory as much as place. He did his best to keep it from showing in his face. "They water their fields from the river," he observed.

"Only river worthy of the name for a hundred *li* in any direction," Chagatai said. "Although I confess I've never ridden west of here to see for myself."

"Their city has no walls, no defenses." As their horses filled up the paddock, Shono climbed atop the fence for a better view. "And no horses to speak of. Some camels."

"Their warriors are brave enough, but the Hidden Valley's true defenders are the hundreds of li of desolation all around them. Even their river gives up and runs into dry clay only a little way downstream, in the dry season."

"But the Sand Road leads straight here."

"In times of peace, yes," said Ide Ryōma. "I understand the Ganzu have a few tricks they can employ if they fear an enemy may approach along the Sand Road."

Iuchi Shoan, who stood up in her stirrups and squinted upstream toward the river's source, murmured half to herself, "Some magic, too, I shouldn't wonder." The shugenja had passed most of the ride in silence, and Chagatai laughed aloud.

"She speaks!" he chuckled. "And not just to the spirits!"

Shoan's brow wrinkled, and she turned her attention to the Moto. "Do you always treat your elders so disrespectfully, Chagatai-kun?" she asked. "Perhaps I'd be more willing to speak to you if you had anything of interest to say." She clucked her tongue and steered her horse toward the path down into the valley.

"If I didn't know better," said Chagatai as he followed, "I'd think that Shoan-sama didn't like me."

Shono nudged Tsubasa after Daichin. "Ryōma-san, tell me more of the Ganzu."

"The Ganzu were happy to swear fealty to Shinjo Khulan Khan in 1010," said Ide Ryōma. "But they were forced to surrender to the caliph in 1072 when he attempted to conquer the Sand Road. The better part of their warriors marched east and joined with the White Horde and the Battle Maidens, who broke the Nehiri advance and reclaimed the lost land in 1074."

"And *only* the lost land," grumbled Chagatai. "The Shinjo khan forbade the sacking of al-Zawira then, and so the Moto stayed their hand. Had I been khan, the caliph would have been cast down and his city made a warning to those who would raise a hand against us." He swung down from Daichin and led the stallion into the paddock.

"And then the Unicorn would trade with whom, precisely?" Ryōma asked, dismounting his shaggy dun, Patience.

"Some new king would rise in the region to trade with, I am certain." Chagatai waved a dismissive hand. "And there's still the Ivory Kingdoms."

"Ryōma-san, you said the Ganzu *marched* to join the White Horde?" said Shono. "On foot?"

"The Ganzu are a hardy people. Some of them survived."

Shono looked at the smiling people around him, bowing to him as they went about their business. *My people, when I am khan.* He saw Chagatai stretch expansively and then swagger toward the center of the village. *Or Chagatai's, if he has his way.* A vision of the Unicorn under Chagatai Khan swam in Shono's mind: war on all fronts, a harvest worthy of the Ujik's Lords of Death. *It would be easier for me to let Chagatai take my place, to shirk my duty. But Bushidō commands otherwise. Duty, Loyalty, Righteousness—they forbid me to step aside.* But did they also command him to do so? Should there be no consequence for Mitsuko's blood on his hands?

"Come!" said Chagatai. "The Ganzu khan will want to make us welcome. It will be nice to sleep in a proper bed again; these houses are no yurts, but they're better than the dusty ground!"

They walked on one of the valley's elevated roads, making their way toward the only buildings Shono could see that rose above the flat plain of the general plan. One Shono took for the daimyō's manor, if daimyō was the term to use for the Ganzu leader. The other's dome-shaped roof suggested it was some sort of temple. He stepped back to where Iuchi Shoan walked, threading prayer beads through her fingers. "Auntie," he said. "To which god is that temple dedicated? Surely the Ganzu do not honor the kami?"

Shoan shook her head. "No, Shono-san. They follow a new gaijin tradition. Followers of that faith are called Qamarists, and you will see many of them when we reach al-Zawira; this caliph you ride to treat with calls himself the Protector of the Qamarist Faith."

"Who or what is Qamar? A god?"

"As to that, you will have to ask a Qamarist priest. My knowledge does not extend to the matter."

Chagatai was right: they slept well that night. The next day, they remained in the Hidden Valley as guests of Ganzu Hama, the daimyō, or khan—in the local language, the *khutun*. She received Shono, Yumino, and Ryōma in her garden in the cool morning light shortly after they broke their fast.

The khutun was a small woman, her hair grey and her spotted hand clutched around the head of an ebony cane. She was dwarfed by the heavy-laden fruit trees of her garden, hobbling along beneath them as if in some far-off forest and not in a tiny square of earth surrounded on all sides by her palace. But this tiny woman from a tiny family had no fear of treating Shono as if he were an errant grandson. "It has been many years since a member of the Great Khan's family deigned to visit my valley," she said, leaning on her cane.

"My mother sends her respects," Shono said. "I know that she would be very glad to visit your city and see its wonders for herself, if the war and matters of court did not detain her." It was probably even true. He had often heard Altansarnai Khan lament that her duties did not permit her to travel as much as she would like.

"Yes, your war," Hama tsked. "A shame. Though I hear that you have made a name for yourself on the battlefield."

"News travels swiftly," Shono said. "But I fear it is exaggerated. My warriors and I won a battle, nothing more."

"And killed the woman to whom you had been betrothed to do it. Not many would have the stomach for such a thing."

Mitsuko filled his vision, screaming, knocking Taka aside and killing his horse. She came for him, for Shono—their blades clashed. His sword plunged into her stomach.

That was then. Focus on now, you fool.

"The betrothal was broken when Matsu Mitsuko attacked Hisu Mori Toride," said Yumino. "My lord Shono's duty was clear. His course was decided, and his honor demanded he follow it."

Was that for Hama Khutun's benefit, or for mine? And how long had he been silent, lost in his memory, that Yumino had felt compelled to speak for him?

"Honor," observed the khutun. "And was it honor that caused your mother to break her engagement and give the Lion the excuse they needed to attack in the first place?"

Ryōma bowed deeply. "The fault belongs to the Ide. The treaty said 'according to custom,' and we understood that to mean according to the custom of Rokugan, where the samurai of the lesser family joins the greater. But the Ikoma insisted after the treaty was signed that it meant *Ikoma* custom, where the bride joins the groom's family. A dreadful oversight on our part."

"Hmph," snorted Hama. "You mean that the Lion believe their daimyō outranks our Khan of Khans."

"My mother would have been forced to abdicate her post," Shono said.

"And all of Rokugan would see that the Unicorn are no better than a vassal family, in the eyes of the Great Clans," said Yumino.

"Instead, all of Rokugan sees that the Shinjo break their word, then task the Ide to take the blame," boomed Chagatai from atop the garden wall. He took a step to a nearby ladder, then slid down it to join them.

Yumino stiffened at Shono's side. Her hand had a stillness to it as if she were very carefully refraining from gripping her sword.

Chagatai may not have sent the Tegensai to kill me, but he has just stabbed me in the heart. Shono's nostrils flared as he took a deep breath, seeking stillness. The sweet summer smell of the garden and the richness of black earth filled him, along with the leathery tang of Chagatai. "What would you have done in my mother's place, Cousin?" *What would I have done?* "Bowed your head, let your clan be diminished?"

Chagatai grinned like a wolf. "I would have marched right into my wedding day and come out with Ikoma Anakazu's head for thinking he could cheat the Unicorn."

"So my cousin objects to the way in which Altansarnai Khan broke the engagement," said Shono. "He finds it insufficiently treacherous and bloody-minded."

"Does not Bushidō command us to commit fully to our course of action?" laughed Chagatai. "There's no sense in betrayal by half measures, not if your honor is already forfeit."

"I shall keep your words in mind, Chagatai-san." *For the day when you betray me.*

The Ganzu daimyō insisted they spend a full two days as her guests. Shono would sooner have ridden on immediately, but their herd—especially Umeboshi—was exhausted. *Every day I am gone is another day for the war to turn against the Unicorn. Another day for friends and family to die,* he thought. And then: *And yet you are half-hoping you never return. Make up your mind, Shono.* Agony to be away from his clan, agony to return to them.

He instructed Tanaka and Suke to see that the horses were well watered and fed and given a chance to recover. Though Suke was still cold, he at least did as he was told.

Shono sat quietly in his place of honor at the khutun's right hand during the dinner on their final night. Chagatai, at the khutun's left, was the center of attention. He told his own version of the battle at the way station, one in which each Unicorn left a dozen dead and dying bandits at their feet. Yumino ground her teeth and glared, even when Chagatai spared a few phrases to describe the terror she inspired in the Tegensai as she danced atop the cistern. She did not relent until Chagatai described Shono's bareback charge as demonstrating "courage worthy of a Moto." *But not of a khan.* Chagatai was walking a careful path, lifting up everyone around him, but himself more than the rest. *Was he tutored in the fine Moto art of boasting, or does it come naturally?*

Ganzu Hama laughed and applauded Chagatai's tales from atop her ebony throne. Each armrest was carved in the shape of a lion-dog resting a paw atop a pomegranate. The wall hangings were a mixture of silk and wool, eastern and western materials combined, and all the furnishings were of excellent quality, but with disparate styles so haphazardly juxtaposed they left Shono unsteady on his feet. The manners of the Ganzu were the same: some of the reserved formality of a Rokugani court along with the easy laughter of the Ujik and some other habits that Shono took to be of western influence. *They are a people of the crossroads. More Unicorn than the Shinjo, in some ways, although they are no horsemen. They explore by letting the world come to them.*

He said as much to the khutun in a quiet moment the next morning. The old woman had accompanied them to the paddock and was leaning on her ebony cane as Shono checked Tsubasa's tack.

"You are perceptive, Shono-san," said Hama. "We have been Unicorn only a short time by the standards of the other families in our clan, I know. And even the Moto are treated as outsiders and newcomers in Rokugan. But it is more than an accident of geography that binds us to the Unicorn Clan. Not every tribe in this region joined with Shinjo Khulan Khan willingly."

"How often do you leave this valley?" Shono asked.

"Rarely. We do not grow enough extra grain to support great herds of horses and camels, especially through the dry season when the river slows to a muddy trickle. But there is no way to cross the Burning Sands, in either direction, without stopping at our holy river. People have been coming to this valley for as long as cities have risen on either end of the Sand Road. And they will continue to do so until those cities fall."

No time soon, I trust. Shono mounted, still considering. Chagatai fell in beside him as they clattered across the bridge to the western bank.

"Surely your duties are discharged now, Cousin," Shono said.

"Not at all," said Chagatai. "Your mother charges the White Horde with the defense of the western border, and the Unicorn claim all the land to the edge of al-Zawira. I will ride with you the whole way, Shono-kun!"

Shono let Yumino's steady glare speak for him.

3. The Dead City and the Crooked City

Far-off al-Zawira
Lies now where we once made war.
Nothing of those kings still stood
Paid in full for Shinjo's blood.

The Burning Sands changed color as they rode, from red, to black and yellow, to a blowing, drifting gold. The final passage was the hardest; were it not for the way stations with their cisterns, half of Shono's horses would have died. After only a few hours of the unfettered sun, Shono adopted the loose head wrapping of the Ganzu and found that it helped. Most of the party soon followed suit. They shared a way station with a Nehiri caravan one evening. Every member of the Rokugani contingent bought a cloth of clean white cotton to wrap around their head. Shono had never loved an article of clothing so much in his life.

A simple pleasure, but even those have escaped me since Mitsuko's death. He clung to it, to any sign that things were returning to normal—that he was returning to normal. *Bushidō insists I maintain face in the presence of tragedy. My duty makes no allowances for grief. So I will feel none.* He nearly convinced himself. If nothing else, he was too hot and tired to think about anything else.

Soon enough, they crested their final wave in the sea of dunes and saw the shining ribbon of the King's River wending its way from west to southeast. On the southern bank lay green fields and orchards at least as lush and vibrant as those of the Hidden Valley, all the more inviting for the blistering heat of the day. On the northern bank lay only drifting sand and baked clay, with a few clusters of buildings, most of those ruins.

Where the river crooked from west to south rose a city that sprawled out of sight into the distance, its bright banners and painted domes glimmering in the sun. *It must be twice the size of Khanbulak. It must be larger than Otosan Uchi, the Forbidden City.*

"Al-Zawira," Ryōma pronounced beside him. "Seat of the caliphs for the past six centuries. Our most important partner in trade for the past two."

"What do they all eat?" wondered Chagatai, for once quieted by the spectacle of it.

"The Nehiri have all the land between the King's River and the Queen's River, some hundred li farther south, irrigated and blooming." Ryōma shrugged. "They call this region the Cradle of the World. I call it the World's Garden."

Behind him, Shono heard Shoan gasp. "Auntie?" He turned to see her gesturing to a cluster of ruins on the near bank, her hand clutching a prayer talisman so fiercely he wondered that neither broke.

"I recognize some of those symbols. That's foul sorcery."

"That," said Ryōma, "is the Dead City, and it's where we will be making our camp."

Of course it is. "I trust there is some reasonable explanation for this?" Shono asked as they rode closer.

"This was once part of the Empire of Rempet, dominated by sorcerer-kings and self-proclaimed children of the sun. When Shinjo was here almost a thousand years ago, she cast down the sorcerer-kings and destroyed their idols. It was thanks to our efforts that the Nehiri were set free from bondage and rose to create their own empire in the World's Garden."

"I suppose the locals avoid the place for fear of some curse or another?" asked Shoan. A massive statue—a radiant sun flanked by spreading wings—loomed above them as they rode, as much a promontory or cliff as a work of art.

"No one will trouble us here," Ryōma agreed. "And it serves as a regular reminder of the might and generosity of the Unicorn to periodically renew our claim."

Within the broken walls, Ryōma took charge, directing servants and samurai to caches of supplies buried under drifting sand. Shono found a broken old statue to stand on, letting his hair blow in the cool breeze off the river while Ryōma worked. He stood and watched the city shimmer in the heat, its colors shining and bright. *I've never seen a city like this before. Hardly anyone in Rokugan has.*

Something about the thought sat ill with him. *In Rokugan, peasants die in the same village they're born in, seldom venturing more than a few dozen li in any direction. Even samurai rarely travel outside their clan's dominion.* Of his party, not even Ryōma had ridden this far west before.

"When was the last Unicorn mission here, Ryōma-san?" asked Shoan as the encampment sprung up around them.

"Two years gone, Shoan-sama," said Ryōma. "With no official Imperial sanction, we dare not maintain a permanent embassy here, but we visit often enough to warrant storing some supplies in the Dead City."

"Who led that delegation?" Shono asked.

"Ide Ashijun, before his ascension to Emerald Magistrate. Most of what I know of the situation here comes from his notes."

"And it's safe?" asked Yumino. Her hand hadn't left her sword since they'd passed beneath the crumbling sandstone arch at the city's edge.

"There's nothing here but sand, rock, and a few broken statues," said Ryōma. "Just be sure to check your boots for scorpions in the morning." He climbed up on the broken statue to stand at Shono's side. "My lord, will you ride directly to the caliph?"

"Is that what you recommend, Ryōma-san?"

"Yes, my lord."

"Then we shall do so."

"Ha," boomed Chagatai. "Well, then let's go."

"Not you," said Shono.

"Eh?" The burly Moto halted halfway through his turn toward the horses.

"You are not part of this diplomatic mission, Chagatai-san." *For which we can all be thankful.* "If you will stay, stay, but I charge you to guard the camp."

"Hmmm," growled Chagatai. For a moment, Shono thought he would refuse. *Nothing is wrong. He will obey. You will treat with the caliph, and all will be well.* "It will be done," Chagatai said eventually. He stalked away, calling for his lieutenants.

"Ryōma-san, you will accompany me." *So that I don't wind up one foot in the stirrups, but of course we don't mention that. Face. Confidence.*

"Of course." Ryōma bowed.

Shono turned and found Yumino sitting astride her dapple grey, Kiso, with Umeboshi's reins in one hand and Ryōma's shaggy little beast Patience on her other side. *Of course Yumino will not allow herself to be left behind.* "Then let us waste no time, Shono-sama."

"Kiso is high-spirited," Shono observed as he mounted. "Is he the best choice for a city?"

"He will not enjoy it," Yumino admitted. "But as your yōjimbō, I wish to have my best weapons at my disposal in the event of any attack, and Kiso is one of the blessed herd. By any measure, an Utaku steed is a battle maiden's best weapon."

"Then we must honor Kiso's sacrifice," said Ryōma as he mounted Patience. "Let us all pray to the ancestors that our mission is successful."

Shono reached for a prayer and found nothing. Instead, he simply led them up the slope and out of the encampment.

"What is our mission, precisely, Ryōma-san?" Yumino asked. "If I do not overstep to ask."

"Our war with the Lion complicates our relationship with Caliph Harun al-Hakim," Ryōma said from somewhere beneath his hat. "Lord Shono's charge is to ensure that the caliph remains our friend and doesn't seek to take advantage of our distraction. The last thing Altansarnai Khan wants is a war on two fronts."

"Is the caliph a man to be cowed by force, or won by flattery?" Yumino wondered.

"An excellent question. And so you see why this is a task only the son of the Khan of Khans could attempt, for he has both arrows in his quiver."

Do I? "It seems to me that my arrows are a breeding pair of Shinjo horses, a fine silk gown, and two trained hunting falcons." He turned in his saddle to see that the gifts were following, Ryōma holding the lead rope. "The caliph is a rich man. Whatever it is he wants, these gifts are surely not it."

"The gifts are necessary, and you're forgetting a hundredweight of tea," said Ryōma. "But you are correct. Our better hope is that the khan sends her son and heir to treat with the caliph. That's a mark of great respect."

"And Shono-sama is a great warrior, as well," Yumino added. "His victory at Hisu Mori Toride secures his reputation."

Mitsuko dying as the wind threw embers into the sky. "You are magnificent in battle, Shono," she said.

Shono put his heels to Boshi's flanks and broke into a gallop.

4. The First Audience

An Ide rode to Uchi-san
In the summer when days were long.
He waited for an audience there
And rode home with snow in his hair.

The bridge into the city was an oddity. Flat-topped barges floated atop the river, lashed together into a single path. Camels laden with goods from desert tribes, Nehiri warriors with their faces hidden beneath black scarves, white-clad pilgrims in billowing robes all walked across the bridge as if it were solid ground. At the fore and aft of each barge was mounted a curving prominence of gilded wood, hung with a lantern, and beneath the deck of the bridge slept or lounged a bargeman with a long pole.

"The Bridge of Boats," Ryōma proclaimed. "It can be dismantled if an invader or flood threatens and is easily reassembled when the danger has passed."

None of their horses passed over the bridge eagerly, but they put up only modest protests. Even Kiso offered only a flick of the ears to show his displeasure.

"I presume our caliph lies within," Shono said, gesturing to the towering white walls perhaps a li away.

"Indeed," said Ryōma. "That's the Round City, the oldest and most prestigious district in all of al-Zawira." He peeked out from beneath his hat and grinned, and Shono was reminded that his language tutor was not much older than him. "Also the roundest."

The city was a confusion of scents, sights, and sounds that exceeded anything in Shono's experience. The spices of cooking food, the smoke of burning incense, and the stink of a great mass of humans and animals all living atop one another was enough to leave him nose-blind. The constant dull roar—of merchants hawking their wares, lovers quarreling in gardens, donkeys braying in the streets, the faithful raising their voices in prayer, musicians playing their beautiful creations, even the sparking cough of fireworks streaking into the sky—overwhelmed his Shinjo-trained sense of hearing as well.

And the people! Black-skinned Bandar and pale-skinned Suhilim and people of every shade in between. Nehiri with their long robes and brightly colored head scarves, Sogdans with the brilliant patterns on their long coats, and other peoples Shono could only gape at, each in clothing and adornment more unusual than the last. One tall, pale man with hair the color of copper had an outlandish ruff of lace around his neck. A woman with skin the color of unfired clay had brilliant jewels embedded in her nose and ears, with a golden chain running between them. A lean man with what looked to be tattooed writing crawling all over his face and naked arms capered and danced, while a small whirlwind with burning eyes of fire spun and pranced alongside him to the music of two pipes in the man's mouth. Al-Zawira made the diversity and splendor—and the squalor—of Khanbulak look like a candle before the sun.

Yumino stared straight ahead as they rode. Ryōma again looked half-asleep in his saddle, but by slight shifts in his shoulders Shono surmised he was studying the crowd as intensely as he was. *It's a sort of freedom. Riding into the endless plain, or vanishing into the mass of humanity. Either way, I could go and never return.* It was a seductive thought. Shono tried not to think it too loudly. *Remember your duty.*

When they approached the walls, guards in steel caps wrapped with black scarves crossed their spears to block their passage through the gates. "Who rides armed to the Round City?" demanded one guard in Nehiri.

Ryōma nudged his horse to the fore. "Shinjo Shono, son of Shinjo Altansarnai of the Unicorn Clan, comes to the Round City to treat with Caliph Harun al-Hakim," he replied in the same language. "We come in peace and bearing gifts."

A woman appeared in the shadows of the gate beneath the mighty walls. "And you are greeted in peace, Shono ibn Altansarnai al-Shinjo." Her voice was thunder and honey, commanding attention like the oncoming storm, yet she herself was nothing more than a shadow, with two eyes glowing like a cat's in the darkness. "Please," she said. "Follow me."

They passed through the gate and rode for several long, echoing seconds beneath the wall. When they emerged into the light, Shono at last had a chance to study her. She was tall—taller than him—a bright slash of color against the black uniforms of the guards. Her robe was saffron-orange with a black fringe, and she wore gold at her ears, throat, and waist. Deep-red garnets sparkled on her bronze fingers, and her eyes were like liquid gold.

"The stables are here," she said, gesturing just beyond a number of tall, muscular servants. "Please, allow them to take your horses."

Shono dismounted and handed Boshi's reins wordlessly to the closest servant. The others did the same, and then Ryōma coughed and stepped forward. "These two are gifts for the caliph." He managed to combine gesturing to the horses with removing his hat and bowing. "Would it be proper to leave them here, or to bring them directly to his presence?"

"The caliph does not care to have beasts roam freely through his Inner City," the woman purred. "The servants will ensure all your gifts are delivered to their proper destination."

Ryōma bowed. "Thank you, *sayidah*."

"Let us proceed," she murmured, and they followed her deeper into the Round City, where another set of walls rose above them.

The silence as they walked in the woman's shadow grew deeper and more awkward. Ryōma was in agony, eyes wide, hat turning a slow circle in his hands. Yumino seemed unimpressed, the classic cool and collected Utaku as she watched everything with glimmering, dark eyes. Shono sought something to say to break the silence.

Their arrival at the gate beneath the inner walls suggested a topic. He gestured above them. "These walls are impressive."

"They are," the woman agreed. "Built in the second century. There is no other wall to equal it in all the world."

"The Kaiu Wall in Rokugan is taller," said Shono. "And longer, by hundreds of li."

"I am certain the Shinjo prince has seen many large and strong walls in his life." As they proceeded into the shadows beneath the wall again, the woman seemed to vanish in the darkness, only her golden eyes and the flash of her smile visible. "But you misunderstand. The walls are celebrated in the Caliphate for their impressive feat of describing a perfect circle." In the dim light, the garnets on her fingers sparked as she traced a circle with both hands. "Two of your li across, and perfectly round." As they emerged into the light again, Shono saw that she was smiling. "I will let you decide if this feat is worthy of the celebration it enjoys."

"As you say," Shono said. "You called me a prince. I fear you are mistaken; we reserve such a title for those of Imperial blood. Perhaps your language makes no such distinction?"

"If you are to treat with the caliph as an equal," said their guide, "then a prince you shall be."

Shono glanced over his shoulder, to where Ryōma was doing his best to remain serene. *The caliph raises my status, to raise his own.* Shono thought of Chagatai.

"And what is your role here, my lady?" Shono asked. "Are you a princess?"

The woman laughed, and Shono had a sudden impression of a stalking tiger. "Hardly. I am called Mandana. I serve the caliph as his chief advisor."

"And your family? Your people?"

"I am Mandana bint No One al-Nowhere. Just Mandana."

"To rise to your position is no easy feat for a woman from Nowhere," said Shono. "The caliph must value your advice highly."

"All who hear me speak value my advice," Mandana said, her voice a velvet purr. Shono could well believe it. He half wondered if there was some sorcery behind her words, to hold his attention so. *The sorcerer-kings are dead and gone. Shinjo-no-Kami killed them.*

"I have heard you called the Tiger Woman," said Ryōma. "Your fame spreads even to Rokugan."

Does it? Shono wondered. *It is the first I have heard of her.*

Mandana smiled, just like a predatory cat, all teeth and no warmth. "I like that. It makes me sound very dangerous. But have no fear, *sadah*. You are safe from me while you are guests of the caliph."

Beyond the wall, the confusion of tightly packed but elegant houses on either side gave way to sprawling palaces and manor houses, gardens alive with calling birds and babbling fountains. The avenue before them ran toward a tremendous building surmounted by a blue dome that sparkled in the sun. Other avenues ran to join it, spokes of a wheel running toward the axle. "The Grand Temple," Mandana said. "Built in the fourth century. It is the largest Qamarist temple anywhere, even larger than those in the City of God."

"Is it where I am to meet the caliph?"

"The caliph has many palaces," Mandana said. "Today he receives you in the Judge's Court. It is on our right, just here," and indeed, they had arrived.

More guards stood at the gates to the palace gardens, and as he entered, Shono felt the difference between his home and this strange place with its round walls. The Shinjo were not great keepers of gardens, preferring to do their contemplation on the open plain or in a wild forest, but the gardens Shono had explored in his youth were all carefully manicured to present an illusion of the natural world. Were it not for the paths and lanterns, one might be forgiven for thinking a Rokugani garden was a natural collection of plants and stone. But no such error was possible for the garden in the Judge's Court. Paths ran in straight lines, intersecting at precise angles, and arranged together in a pattern of perfect symmetry. Flowers and trees grew in ordered ranks, the configurations of their colors and perfume mathematical in their perfection. *What do I have to offer someone from such a different world? What is it he wants?*

Shono paused a moment in the garden. "Do you enjoy gardens, my prince?" asked Mandana.

Memories rose, as clear and fragrant as the flowers around him: Mitsuko, racing through the garden in her uncle's estate. Laughter. The thrill of evading her maids and nurse, together. *We were fourteen?* He put the thought aside. *Nothing is wrong. I will not allow my musings to distract from my duty.*

"Less than I once did," Shono said. "Take me to the caliph, if you please, Mandana-sama." She smiled as he used the Rokugani honorific despite speaking Nehiri, then led him to the doorway. A carpet hung across it in lieu of a door.

"The caliph awaits."

Shono bowed and entered, Ryōma at one side, Yumino scowling at the other. They passed under the arch into a long gallery, light and airy with tall empty windows on two sides.

Mandana stepped forward and announced them, her voice swelling to fill the entire hall. "Presenting His Excellency Shono ibn Altansarnai al-Shinjo, prince of the Unicorn Clan, Noyan of the Blue Horde, and heir apparent to the khan."

Seeing no place to remove his boots, Shono led the others in a steady walk down the length of the gallery. Their feet clopped on a mosaic floor of red and white stone. Courtiers, guards, and hangers-on from a dozen nations watched with naked interest as Shono's party crossed the room. *Come gawk at the barbarian. Within Rokugan or without, it seems everyone finds us a spectacle wherever we go.*

The caliph sat at the far end of the gallery atop a small mound of striped cushions. He was a stout man, his hair and beard more grey shot through with black than the other way around. Shono placed his age at nearly sixty and his height at just less than his own. His skin was perhaps a shade darker than Shono's, with a warmer golden tone. Aside from the jewels sparkling at his fingers and throat and the size and magnificence of his turban, Shono might have overlooked him as just another courtier in this far-off land.

Behind him was a collection of people, mostly quite young, mostly quite beautiful. They had skin as fair as porcelain or as deep as Hama Khutun's ebony throne or anywhere in between. They wore Nehiri-style caftans and robes, for the most part, their hair hidden under scarves or turbans or other headdresses. Shono resisted the urge to run a hand through his own loose-flowing hair. *Perhaps I should have made an effort to dress as a local.* He couldn't tell if the caliph's attendants were ornaments or advisors, or perhaps both.

The one closest to him wore a fawn-colored robe, her head wrapped in a scarf of deep burgundy. Her robe was cinched with a belt of gold medallions, and more medallions lay hanging from her throat and resting on her deep-brown forehead. Her eyes shone darkly in the shafts of light streaking in from the windows. Her lips were turned down in an expression of distaste, smoothed into bland serenity as Shono approached.

"That is Saadiyah bint Abdul Rahim al-Mozedu," murmured Mandana at Shono's side, matching him stride for stride. *Saadiyah, daughter of Abdul Rahim, of Mozedu,* Shono translated. "Watch out for her, *sayid.* You have no friends in this court save perhaps for me, and she is the cleverest of the caliph's little birds and has no reason to love the Unicorn."

If Mandana is my closest friend in this court, I may as well throw myself to the wolves. Shono bowed before the caliph as Mandana climbed the dais to stand one step below the most powerful man in the West.

"You stand before Harun ibn Mahmour ibn Ja'far al-Hakim, Caliph, Defender of the Faith, Sultan of al-Zawira, Beloved by God, and Supreme Leader of the Qamari Peoples," she said, her voice ringing throughout the audience hall.

Shono straightened, and his eyes fell on Saadiyah and her penetrating, considering gaze from beneath her burgundy head covering. Unbidden, Mitsuko leapt to his mind. *Our first meeting, that look of dubious contempt. To think that we would go from that, to love, to war.* "Great sultan," Shono began.

"Caliph," murmured Ryōma.

"Great caliph," Shono amended. *Put Mitsuko from your mind. A samurai does his duty; he does not moon about after lost love.* "I bring gifts from my mother, the Champion of the Unicorn Clan, daimyō of the Shinjo, and Khan of Khans." Servants stepped forward, and he found his tongue, speaking with more confidence than he felt. "We offer two trained hawks, for I understand falconry is a sport beloved by both our peoples. I had the training of one of these birds myself; my mother trained the other. Let the speed and keen vision of a hawk on the wing represent always your great wisdom and mercy."

A low murmur spread through the assembly. *But is it approval, or dismay?* He carried on as a servant presented the next gift. "We offer a gown of the finest silk, woven and sewn by artisans of the Crane Clan, the finest in the Emerald Empire. We hope that this priceless treasure may find favor with all your court." The gown had been made to order according to the specifications of some Ide expert or another, possibly Ryōma. Its sky-blue silk was embroidered with gold thread and studded with pearls. It even seemed that it might fit the caliph's stout frame adequately well.

With a thump, two servants placed a chest between them at the caliph's feet. Shono bowed as the servants opened the chest for all to see. "And finally, a hundredweight of the finest tea in the Emerald Empire. Let it be a warm reminder of the riches that both our peoples gain when we trade freely along the bountiful Sand Road."

The servants closed the chest again, and it, along with all the other gifts, vanished into the crowd. The caliph frowned down the length of his hawklike nose at Shono and stroked his beard.

Mandana broke the silence with a soft purr. "Prince Shono is forgetting the most priceless of his gifts, a fine breeding pair of Shinjo horses. I had the pleasure of seeing them stabled in the Middle City."

"Curious," said Saadiyah. Her voice had none of Mandana's power, but it rang clear and steady like a bell. "Has Prince Shono perhaps forgotten that it was our horses in the Cradle of the World that enriched their bloodline and made them what they are today? Does he imagine that our herds are in need of improvement?"

"Now, sister, mind your words," said Mandana with another smile. "You speak of 'our horses' as if you or any Bandar were there all those centuries ago."

"Naturally not, my lady," said Shono. He cast about for some perfect words to say. "Our horses are as much a symbol of Unicorn esteem as a treasure in their own right. I would not presume to advise your own horse breeders of their business, but in any case, adding our horses to your herds remains a symbol of friendship between our two peoples."

The caliph spoke at last. "You speak of two peoples," he said in a wheezy voice. "Which two? Shinjo and Nehiri? Rokugani and Qamarist? I think perhaps the situation is more complex than that."

"I'm certain I do not know what you mean," said Shono, truthfully.

"Perhaps not," said Harun. "Perhaps we shall discuss it in more detail at a later date. But you must be tired and hungry from the road." He clapped his hands, and Mandana, Saadiyah, and all the rest of his attendants bowed as he rose. "Let us retire to the Dancer's Palace for dinner and amusements."

The entire court assembled, swiftly and according to some protocol Shono could not ascertain, into a procession. First came a small, perfumed man with a great parasol, which he carried above the caliph's head. Next went the caliph, flanked by two guards in coats of gold brocade. Shono found himself walking between Saadiyah and Mandana, a startling and unsettling pair of escorts to be sure. Saadiyah made no effort to hide her appraisal as she studied him or to hide her dismay at what she saw. Mandana, on the other hand, barely could be bothered to spare him a glance. Yumino and Ryōma were both gone, lost in the parade. "Is it normal for the caliph to shift to a new palace for a meal?" he asked.

"As I said, the caliph has many palaces," murmured Mandana. "And as a great lover of palaces, he uses each according to its particular strengths."

"Be glad that our procession today takes us through the Silver Garden," said Saadiyah. "You have no such wonders in your kingdom, I believe."

Fortunes bless and preserve me, she is worse than a Crane. She might as well call me "barbarian" while she's at it.

Shono glanced about as the procession snaked through a round gate and stepped down into a grotto hidden from the avenue outside by an intricately carved screen. The garden within was a lush profusion of green plants and murmuring fountains, and the whistles and trills of unfamiliar birds perfumed the air as surely as the colorful flowers blooming everywhere Shono looked. "It is a fine enough garden, I allow, but—"

"Just wait." Mandana smiled.

"Have no fear, foreigner," said Saadiyah. "The Silver Garden has yet to display its principal treasure."

Ah, there it is. "Foreigner."

A few paces later, the procession passed through an arch of blooming trees and came into a large central court, as perfectly square, Shono assumed, as the Round City was perfectly circular. In the center rose a tremendous tree that glimmered in the evening light. Every leaf, every bough, shone with reflected sun and lantern light, glimmering at turns silver and gold as Shono's perspective shifted. Perched on the tree everywhere he looked were birds of gold, with feathers of precious stones, each bobbing and singing and trilling in a complex symphony. The limbs of the tree rustled as if stirred by a breeze, though the air was still, and water trickled along its roots, giving only a hint as to the intricate mechanism that allowed the whole to function.

"The great tree of the Silver Garden is made from over a ton of precious metals," Saadiyah proclaimed proudly, her gaze fixed firmly on the improbable tree. "The finest philosophers and engineers from throughout the Qamarist world worked together on its design."

"It isn't sorcery, then?" asked Shono.

"Not at all," Saadiyah said. "The ingenuity of humankind alone is responsible for this wonder. The engine is powered by the flow of water."

Both women seemed to be awaiting some sort of response from him. Shono wondered what he should feel: awestruck wonder, as Saadiyah seemed to expect? Or amusement, as Mandana fairly radiated? He felt neither. *Your tree is very nice, but I am numb inside because I slew my betrothed in battle* is not something a samurai should say. "It is magnificent," he said at length.

Soon they were all arranged again in the Dancer's Palace, where long tables formed three sides of a square, and all the diners sat on the outside edge. Shono was directed to a seat between Saadiyah and Mandana again. The other guests each sat cross-legged on a cushion, but Shono set his cushion aside and sat in the Rokugani fashion. Yumino, who had been seated at the utter edge of the horseshoe to his right, did the same, but Ryōma, only a few seats past the caliph to his left, sat on the cushion as if he'd done so all his life.

Once everyone was seated, the caliph clapped his hands again, and silence fell. "We welcome our guests from across the Burning Sands, may God the Comforter shelter them," he called. "And we offer these tokens of our esteem."

A flood of servants emerged, each bearing a gift. The first approached Shono and bowed low, presenting a jeweled scabbard with a gold-chased hilt emerging from it. Shono glanced at Ryōma, who nodded slightly. *This isn't Rokugan. Refusal is neither expected nor required.*

"I thank you, great caliph," Shono said, taking the sword and drawing it. The steel seemed to flicker in the fading light of the day, ripples of dark and light flowing down the blade. *Blood would scarcely show against that pattern.* Its balance in his hand was perfect. *This sword has never killed anyone I loved. It's more than I can say for my own blade.* "It is exquisite," he remembered to say after a time.

"The secret of watered steel is known only to Qamari smiths," proclaimed the caliph. "There is no other steel like it in all the world for strength and flexibility."

There followed gift after gift. A tunic so dense with gold brocade it stood on its own atop the cushion. A magical amulet, proof against any poison, from Mandana. A saddle of exotic wood, leather, and ivory. Gold medallions for his belt. A dagger whose hilt was carved jade. Yumino and Ryōma were not forgotten, either; a silver tea set and cups in gaijin style for Ryōma, gold and jewels for Yumino. With each gift, Shono fumbled for his courtesies while the caliph boasted of its extravagance.

At last, only one gift remained: a tiny, intricate bird fashioned from white gold. Purple amethysts served for its eyes, and delicate ivory feathers adorned its ruff. A golden key protruded from its side. "You are meant to turn the key," suggested Saadiyah, as if guiding a child. Shono swallowed his annoyance and did so. The bird turned its head, fluttered its wings, and sang a liquid flow of soaring beauty.

"It is beautiful," admitted Shono. "And cleverly made. This is akin to the birds in your Silver Garden?"

"The caliph's Silver Garden," Saadiyah said. "But yes."

For some reason, Shono thought of his exchange of gifts with Mitsuko, when their betrothal was formalized. He had given her the very finest horse in his stable. She had given him a copy of Akodo's *Leadership* that had been in her family more than six hundred years. *I sent it back to her mother. I wonder if it arrived before or after I sent her Mitsuko's corpse?*

"You do not care for it?" Saadiyah asked. "Perhaps it is too delicate for your nomadic ways?" Shono glanced at her, startled from his memories.

What must my face have looked like? "I admire this gift intensely," he said. "Forgive my rudeness. My journey has been long."

"In that case"—Mandana smirked—"I apologize for what you are about to endure."

"For shame, Mandana," chided Saadiyah. "To speak so ill of the caliph's entertainments."

"Does not the Prophet command honesty?" asked Mandana with perfect innocence.

"What great trial must I now brave?" Shono asked, setting the jeweled bird aside. One of the servants whisked it away, as they had all the previous gifts.

"Dinner," said Saadiyah.

Dinner proceeded through over a dozen courses, and each course was accompanied by its own folly or performance. First, a man emerged with a strange instrument, like a *biwa*, and sat and warbled at the assembly. Then came another man, naked from the waist up, who flourished a variety of swords, then swallowed each sword to its hilt. Two women were next, who gyrated their bare stomachs as they danced. Meanwhile, Shono was served a plate of olives, then a round of bread and a dish of aromatic bean spread, then a delicate flaky grain steamed with pine nuts, then goat stewed with spices and vegetables from the breadth of the Cradle of the World, and on and on. With every course, servants walked among the diners, pouring a fruity purple wine from silver jars.

The caliph set the pace, eating and drinking more than anyone else at the table. Shono found that he had no appetite, and he forced himself to eat a few bites of each new dish for the sake of politeness. *A year ago, I would have enjoyed this feast.* He left his wine untouched, to keep his head as clear as he could manage, and saw that Saadiyah had turned her cup upside down, to prevent the servants from pouring into it. Mandana, Shono noticed, had neither plate nor cup before her and was offered nothing by the servants.

"You are abstaining from the wine?" Shono asked.

"The Prophet warns against the vice of alcohol," Saadiyah said.

"And you, Mandana-sama?" Shono winced as he realized he had just spoken in Rokugani. He made to try again in Nehiri, but Mandana answered as if she had not noticed the gaffe.

"I will eat later. I am here simply to advise the caliph, not to partake of his amusements."

"I see." Shono glanced across the room and past where a dozen beautiful young people were dancing in a most acrobatic fashion. Yumino had her untouched cup of wine to one side, but Ryōma sipped happily as the woman seated next to him laughed at something he had just said. No one else was abstaining from the vice of drink. "It seems your people do not think much of the Prophet's warning, in general."

"The court takes its cues from the caliph," said Saadiyah. "Some previous caliphs have gone so far as to ban wine entirely within the lands where they held sway. Others maintain that the grape is God's creation, and therefore there can be no sin in its enjoyment."

"Harun al-Hakim is from the latter school of thought," said Mandana. "Such liberality makes him popular among the noble classes, and particularly among the vintners."

"A toast!" bellowed the caliph, lifting his great silver cup high. "Shinjo! Raise your cup, to the friendship between the Qamari Empire and the Unicorn Clan!"

"To our lasting friendship," Shono said, with less power and conviction than he had intended. He set the broad silver cup down again as the caliph drank.

When he had swallowed his wine, Harun wiped his beard and mustache with the back of his hand, then turned to study Shono again. "Tell me, Shinjo," he said. "You are your mother's heir, are you not?"

"I am," Shono said.

"Yet you are her youngest son, I am told." *Told by whom? What spies do you have in Unicorn lands?* The caliph gestured with one fat hand, the gems sparkling. "You have an older brother. Is he addled in his wits? Deficient in his manhood? Why are you the heir, and not he?"

Because my brother is too much like you, and would enjoy this feast with its dancing and wine more than I. Shono took a breath. "My brother, Yasamura, has no desire to be the khan, nor do his skills and temperament lend him easily to that role. My mother chose me, instead."

"But he was firstborn," said Saadiyah. "Chosen by God to be her heir. Who are you, and who is your mother, to set aside the will of God?"

"The kami in their wisdom gave my mother three children," Shono snapped. "She chose the best from among them as her heir." Heat rose in his cheeks, and Shono took a breath. *Calm. This woman is trying to provoke you.*

The caliph grunted and took another swig of his wine. *It could be worse, old man. It could be Chagatai sitting here.*

As he studied the crowd, Shono murmured to Mandana. "The caliph keeps referring to the Qamari. I thought the people of al-Zawira were Nehiri."

It was Saadiyah who answered. "They are, in the main," she said. "But I, as you can see, am not. Nehiri, Suhili, Sogdan, Bandar—these are matters of parentage and geography. But all who follow the teachings of the Prophet are Qamari, and Caliph Harun al-Hakim claims dominion over all Qamarists, as the Prophet's rightful heir."

"I see." *The dome of the temple, rising above the gardens of the Hidden Valley.* "And if some Qamarists owe their fealty to some other empire?"

Saadiyah smiled, elaborately innocent. "Then some might say they are either traitors or infidels."

Oh no.

5. The Second Audience

The white pine forest of Hisu Mori glistens in the snow.

To that place of perfect stillness still my spirit longs to go.

I'll bring my beloved thither and uncover her eyes to show

Her the heart that beats within me, and my love she soon will know.

After dinner, they were escorted to a palace set aside for their use: the Prince's Palace, according to their guide. Their baggage was already in the residence when they arrived, and a small army of servants attempted to help Shono undress before he chased them from the room. *It took me two years to get comfortable with Tanaka. I don't even know these strangers' names.*

With Yumino standing guard in the hallway outside, Shono was alone for the first time in longer than he could remember. He massaged his aching feet, unclasped his belt, and crossed to the window, where a carved screen blocked a clear view from the outside but did little to keep out the gentle night breeze or the moonlight. He sat and breathed in the perfume of the garden outside. *The Nehiri love their gardens nearly as much as the Rokugani, strange as those gardens are.*

He sat and stared at nothing and felt tears well in his eyes. *Every wonder I see I want to share with her. And every time I think of her, delight turns to ash in my mouth.* Was this the first time he had truly been alone with his grief since Mitsuko's death? There was no privacy on the road, and he had spent barely a full day in his mother's camp upon his "victorious" return from the battlefield before being dispatched on this new mission.

"I know her loss must grieve you," she had said, her voice low and gentle. The woman who was both the Champion of the Unicorn and his own mother. Seldom had the difference between the two felt so stark.

"Grieve you." As if Altansarnai Khan could possibly understand. *Grief is for the loss of a loved one. I defeated an enemy in battle, Mother, just as a noyan should, as a samurai should. She may not even be dead.* Mitsuko had been breathing, barely, when he walked away, after all. He had abandoned her to die alone. *Perhaps some brave peasant came to her side and nursed her back to life. Perhaps she yet lives, cloistered at a monastery, just waiting for the war to be over so she can be united with me once more.* He let the fantasy grow, nurtured it, until the sound of footsteps in the hall outside shattered him back to reality.

Shono wiped at his eyes. He stood, wrapping his robe around himself in something resembling decent order. When he turned to the doorway, he found Ide Ryōma kneeling, awaiting his acknowledgment as though he were about to pounce.

"Ryōma-san," said Shono. "Can it wait until morning?"

"Respectfully, my lord Shono, no." Shono gestured, and Ryōma rose, stalking into the room and speaking in a low growl. "We must discuss your frankly dismal performance today and ensure that tomorrow goes more smoothly."

"I am certain I don't know what you mean, Ryōma-san," grated Shono.

"Do you think the caliph didn't notice you failing to drink his toast?" Ryōma slumped to sit atop a cushion, propped up against the wall. His eyes were cast down, his body slouched, just as falsely asleep as he ever was in the saddle. "Did you think that perhaps he was delighted with your obvious boredom with his amusements? Do you think your missteps of the tongue project Unicorn strength? Kami keep us, Shono-sama; your mother gave you this task because you needed time to grieve, but that doesn't mean it's not important!" Ryōma pursed his lip, as if misliking the taste of his own words. *Well, finally someone says it. She sent her broken son away.*

"None of that matters," Shono said.

"Does it not?" Ryōma leaned back, blowing out his lips like an annoyed horse. "His first gift to you was a sword, Shono-sama."

"Should I have refused it?"

Ryōma groaned, sweeping his hat from his head and rubbing at the baldness so revealed. "I do not know. Perhaps it is not your lack of focus that is the problem. Perhaps Altansarnai Khan has given us an impossible task." *When she meant to give me something so easy I couldn't fail.*

"You are my advisor and tutor in these matters, Ryōma-sensei." Shono turned his face to the garden once more. "What do you advise?"

"There will be another audience tomorrow. You must refer to Harun only as the caliph, or the Master of the West. Make no mention of the Qamari Empire or the Qamarists as a people."

"The Ganzu," Shono said.

"Not only them," Ryōma growled. "There's a Qamarist temple outside Khanbulak; did you know? By now, how many of the Ujik follow the creed of the Prophet?"

"I don't know. How many?" *And how many Ide, for that matter?*

"If even one *ordu* is Qamari, the caliph could use them as an excuse for war."

"So what are we to do? Cast down the Qamarist temples, forbid any creed but the Tao of Shinsei? This is not the Unicorn way. Even Moto Chagatai more devoutly favors the Lords of Death than Shintao."

"It is not the Unicorn way," Ryōma agreed. "And in any case, forbidding the Qamarist faith would only hand the caliph all the excuse he craves for a war."

"Then what? A show of strength? Remind him that war with the Unicorn would cost him more than he could hope to gain?"

"Perhaps so. I find myself wishing we had brought Moto Chagatai after all."

He thinks Chagatai is a better warrior than me. "To what end? Chagatai speaks not a word of Nehiri. It took me a month to practice it to your satisfaction, and that after years of study as a child."

"Chagatai can't help but project the threat of violence with every movement he makes. No words would be required." *While I project what, the hollow shell of a man grieving the death of his beloved? Does the fact that I slew her, one of the finest warriors of the Lion Clan, in single combat enter into the matter at all?*

"I think you will find, Ryōma-san, that I can be very violent as well, when need be." Shono found that he had stepped forward, dropped his hand to where his sword would be had he not cast his belt aside.

Ryōma raised his hands, open palms toward Shono. *What am I doing, threatening a pacifist?* "Forgive me, my lord. It is late, and we are both exhausted. Think on what we have discussed. I will apply myself to find some peaceful solution, something other than ceding control of the Sand Road to the caliph." He tugged his hat back into place and himself to his feet, bowed low, and left Shono to his grief.

Shono slept, but not well, and was the last to join the others for breakfast the next morning. The servants, a woman his mother's age with her face hidden behind a red veil and two men with identical perfumed beards, had offered up a meal of olives, figs, and dates, as well as coffee served from Ryōma's new samovar, which the little Ide drank with obvious relish.

"We must keep the Sand Road open," he said, "if only because coffee does not grow in the East."

"I prefer tea," said Yumino, wrinkling her nose over her cup.

"So our gifts were not laced with poison or anything so crude?" Shono asked as he sat.

"No," said Ryōma. "I inspected them all thoroughly. I have, ah, sent that magic amulet on to Iuchi Shoan."

"Wise, Yumino grunted. "I do not trust that Mandana. I think she is a sorcerer."

"Our Iuchi shugenja have learned much from the sorcerers of the West," Ryōma pointed out.

"I do not think Shoan would trust her, either," Yumino said, placing her silver cup on the table.

"I think that Saadiyah is worse," said Shono as he accepted a cup of coffee from one of the bearded servants. The jeweled bird stared at him from where it perched on the table before him. *Should we be speaking so frankly? Is it possible one of these servants speaks Rokugani?*

"She insults you and our entire clan," agreed Yumino. "If she wore a sword at her hip, I would have challenged her to a duel by now."

"Dueling—" began Ryōma.

"Is forbidden only between Unicorn, and only to the death," said Yumino. "Shinjo-no-Kami was the essence of compassion, but she was also a warrior. She understood the demands of honor."

"Speak plainly, please, Yumino-san. Do you have reservations about my honor?" Shono took a fig and nibbled, just as if he didn't fear the Utaku's answer.

"I swore no vow to serve you, my lord," she said. "Battle Maidens never do. We live our honor with actions, not words. That I choose to be at your side says everything I need to say about your honor."

"But," said Ryōma. He popped an olive in his mouth with an impish smile.

"But I see that you are...unbalanced," she said with a cool glare at Ryōma. "You need not be. Shinjo-ue is the one who broke the engagement, not you. Mitsuko is the one who attacked Unicorn lands. You did only as Bushidō required and behaved as well as could be expected. Your loyalty to your clan and your family is proven. You gave Matsu Mitsuko an honorable battle and an honorable death."

"An honorable death is still a death," said Shono. "And a poor betrothal present."

Yumino nodded. "As you say, my lord." She set down her cup and stood. "I will check on our horses while you dress, Shono-sama, if you can spare me."

"What I can't spare is the horses. By all means, ensure they are being well treated." He chewed thoughtfully for a moment after she left. *If only things were so simple.* He envied Yumino her easy confidence, her belief that honor alone was sufficient. *I think the past few weeks have proven that it is not.*

After breakfast, he dressed under the fussing attentions of three servants—*but not the same three as served breakfast; no, we wouldn't want you to learn their names or get comfortable*—and Ide Ryōma. He wore as many of the gifts the caliph had bestowed upon him as he could manage, beginning with the brocade coat, then the new medallions on his belt, and his new sword. "It's not rude to go armed in the caliph's presence?"

"He made no attempt to disarm us yesterday," said Ryōma. "Even Yumino. In any case, he can hardly object to your carrying the sword he gave you." Ryōma himself bore no weapons, not even the wakizashi to which his status as a samurai entitled him. Most Ide subscribed to some version of a pacifistic philosophy, but Ryōma was one of the few who would not even wear a sword, let alone draw it.

So Shono wore the sword, and the rest of his finery, and the three of them proceeded to the caliph's pleasure gardens.

Saadiyah called them "the Gardens of Earthly Paradise" when she met them at the gate. "There is no danger within; your bodyguard can wait here."

Is it stronger to insist she come, or to show that I have no need of her protection? "Yumino-san," he said in Rokugani. "Avail yourself of what pleasures these gardens have to offer. I will call if you are required." She bowed and stepped to the side. Ryōma scurried away to consult with a cluster of courtiers in bright colors, leaving Shono at the mercy of the caliph's advisor.

"Is Sheikha Mandana not joining us today?" Shono asked.

"She will do as she pleases, that one," scoffed Saadiyah. "Come. Let us walk a little in the caliph's garden." She turned and led Shono down a path laid with intricate mosaic patterns, surrounded on all sides by flowering trees a little higher than Shono was tall.

"The caliph seems to have a garden and a palace for every day of the week," Shono observed.

"More than that," laughed Saadiyah. "And more still beyond the city walls." She flicked her fingers dismissively. "Have you no gardens to equal this one in your homeland, Shinjo?"

And so the insults begin. "There is a great variety of beautiful gardens throughout Rokugan," he said carefully. *Shall I boast of our great beauty, far in excess of the caliph's? Or display humility?* He had no easy answer. He settled for honesty. "I suspect which gardens are the most beautiful is a matter of personal choice. The Crane, for example, arrange their gardens just so to achieve perfect balance and harmony. We Shinjo prefer gardens that have a touch of wildness to them, with flowers and trees to remind us of the extent of our journeys. I have heard that the gardens of the Scorpion are dark places, full of secret turnings and hidden grottoes."

"Is there no mathematical principle that guides the arrangement? No symmetry?" For perhaps the first time, Shono could believe he heard some honest curiosity and interest in Saadiyah's voice.

I must be imagining things. "If you are asking whether the gardens of my homeland resemble the gardens of the caliph, they have little in common."

"And which do you prefer?"

Sensing a trap, Shono tried for honesty once more. "In truth, I prefer the open plain to any garden I have ever visited in my life."

"Why, Shinjo, I believe that is the first sensible thing you have said."

"My lady?"

"You prefer the work of God's hand over the efforts of mere mortals. I can scarcely find fault with your opinion." She came to a halt beneath a tall statue of white marble, a djinni contemplating a crow perched on its hand. "Do you know what this statue represents?"

"I recognize the djinni. It resembles illustrations from some of the scrolls my father showed me when I was a boy."

"This is called *The Djinn Hear the Prophet's Word.* The prohibition against speaking the Nameless Prophet's name, to shield him from Name Magic, has often been interpreted to extend to his likeness in works of art. So the crow represents his teachings in many such works."

"The djinn follow the Prophet's Word?" Shono tried to imagine elemental kami who would celebrate the wisdom of Shinsei, a shugenja who would preach to a kami rather than pray to them. He had no success. *Djinn are not just kami by another name. They are something else entirely.*

"Some do. Others reject it, just as with humankind. I show it to you because this statue, this event, the rise of the Prophet's Word— they all came about after the Unicorn Clan toppled the empire of Old Rempet from its position on the Throne of the World."

"That was hundreds of years ago."

"It was indeed," Saadiyah agreed. "But the actions of your ancestors are still keenly felt in the Cradle of the World today. Some still cry out for vengeance, even though the sorcerer-kings were cruel tyrants who enslaved human beings and djinn alike. Others look to the caliph, and they wonder: if the Unicorn toppled one ruler, might they end the reign of another?"

"It's not our way to interfere in the affairs of gaijin kingdoms," Shono said. "My ancestors destroyed Rempet because it stole Shinjo-no-Kami from us. Your caliph need fear no such vengeance unless he commits some similar crime." He let his fingers brush the hilt of his sword, to let the implication linger.

"What crime did Caliph Ali al-Walid commit, that Shinjo Khulan Khan felt compelled to conquer all his lands east of the King's River?"

He was weak when Khulan Khan was strong. "I do not see your people clamoring to dwell on the east bank," Shono said instead. "The people east of the river are not Nehiri. They are Unicorn, and have been for generations."

"But they are also Qamarists," said Saadiyah. She shook her head and raised a finger to forestall his objection. "But all that is beside the point. The history between East and West has been one of mutual neglect punctuated by occasional conquest and war. Is it any wonder the caliph is wary of you, of your intentions?"

"It seems, sayidah, that I should be having this conversation with the caliph."

Saadiyah turned and resumed walking down the garden path. More statues of beasts and djinn arose on either side. A horrible one-eyed giant here, an *ifrit* there, a monstrosity part eagle, part lion, with the face of a human being on the right. "It's best for everyone if conversations with the caliph, may God preserve him, are all worked out beforehand," she said. "You and I can speak more frankly than you and him, without the chance of a diplomatic incident."

"You want to control what the caliph hears and says?" Shono wondered. "Is he your puppet, then?"

Saadiyah laughed, suddenly, a quick sharp bark with little mirth. "He's wild, a force of nature. He can no more be controlled than the storms on the Sea of Jewels. Only pray to God for good weather."

"I wonder which you fear more: the Unicorn, or your own caliph."

"Wonder no more," she said. They had passed beneath a trellis crawling with a flowering vine, and at the end of the long walkway sat Caliph Harun al-Hakim beneath a pavilion of shimmering silk. "It is the caliph, long may he live, whom I fear—whom all Qamarists fear. Who else threatens more ruination than our own ruler? The worst you can do, Shinjo, is storm our city and put us to the sword."

If I didn't know better, I'd think she wanted war between our people. "What is it you wanted from this conversation, my lady?" *Perhaps I don't know better; perhaps war is her aim.*

"I wished to learn the measure of the man who would treat with my caliph," she said. "Is he kind? Cruel? Foolish? Wise? Weak? Strong?"

"And have you reached a conclusion?"

"Foolish. Exactly as I would expect from a barbarian prince."

"If you are so concerned about the militant and warlike Shinjo armies, my lady, you might gentle your tone and choose your words with more care," Shono growled. *A shameful lapse of face,* he chided himself. *Perhaps Yumino had the right idea, and I should challenge her to a duel here and now.*

"Foolish, and easily riled," Saadiyah amended. She turned to look directly at him, arms serenely at her side. "You are wearing the sword the caliph gave you. If you must, draw it and cut me down, and then we will all understand exactly what sort of man you are."

She's right. I'm letting my pride and my grief interfere with my duty. He took a breath, then bowed deeply. "Forgive me, Saadiyah-san. Such an outburst is unbecoming. It is as you said: here we can speak frankly. It was wrong of me to take offense."

Saadiyah blinked. "What is it you want from this conversation, Shinjo?"

"I wish to do my duty. To ensure peace between my people and the caliph."

"Simply done. Cede all claim to the rulership of the people of the Sand Road and let the caliph, God shower blessings upon him, administer trade along its route. You will have peace forevermore."

"You have taken the measure of me, Saadiyah-san," Shono said. "But I have had little opportunity to study the caliph."

Saadiyah cocked her head, reminding Shono of nothing so much as a curious bird—of the jeweled bird perched on his breakfast table. "Is there anything you could learn about the caliph, God protect him, that would induce you to accept such terms?"

"If you believe I would never accept the terms, why offer them?"

"Why indeed," she said, and turned away. With a gesture, she indicated the caliph beneath his pavilion. Harun lifted a golden chalice of wine and laughed at something Shono could not see. "By all means, my prince. Take the measure of the man, but he will not receive you today. The caliph wishes to rest after the exertions of yesterday, and his magnificence is taking his pleasure in these gardens. Should a similar urge take you, servants will prepare a place for you to watch the amusements."

"The fact that the servants have not already done so suggests you know what my response will be. Tell me, my lady. What do you think of your lord?"

"The great and merciful caliph is beloved by God and all his subjects," said Saadiyah without even a trace of hesitation. "His generosity and kindness is matched only by his temperance and diligence."

Shono watched as the caliph spilled wine down his front, spreading a dark purple bruise across the yellow-and-red stripes of his caftan. Harun glanced down at the stain and laughed again, leaning back on his mountain of cushions. "And his wisdom?"

"Is matched only by his patience and firm sense of justice."

"I believe I understand you, my lady." *In meaning if not at all in character.* He bowed and turned to go.

"Prince Shono," she said. He paused. "If it came to war…would you win?"

While fighting the Lion at the same time? Not likely. "My people celebrate the five winds," he said. "North, south, east, and west, and the central wind that blows above them all." He turned to face her and found her head cocked in the same curious-bird pose she had adopted earlier. "We divide our forces into five armies—five hordes—both to celebrate the five winds and, as Shinjo did long ago, during our travels." *And never mind that the Green Horde never returned, or that the Purple Horde stands disbanded except in times of great extremity.*

"It hardly matters how many armies you divide your forces into—"

"In all our previous wars with the Caliphate," Shono said, "no more than two hordes have ever been required." With that, he bowed, and took his leave. Saadiyah watched him go, lips pursed and head cocked to one side.

It did not take Shono long to explore the entirety of the caliph's

garden. A large pool dominated its center, where the caliph's pavilion overlooked a fountain and a small space for dancers and singers to perform. Smaller pavilions ran off to the side, where various
courtiers and functionaries sat on their own, observing the amusements or doing their best to be observed. The caliph was accompanied by several of the same gaggle of young, beautiful attendants
from the earlier audience at the Judge's Court, but no one seemed
to be troubling him with affairs of state. His chief occupations were
drinking wine, eating delicacies offered to him by silent servants,
and laughing or cheering at the performances. *How can a man
behave like this and be counted a great ruler? How can his followers
witness this behavior and simply accept it?* Shono took a breath. His
anger was not with the caliph. He turned away.

Shono found Ryōma sitting under one of the pavilions to the
side with three Nehirim arrayed around a game board of polished
mahogany. The little Ide stood as Shono approached.

"Shono-sama," he said, bowing. "May I please introduce Captain Izad of the caliph's guard." The woman across the board from
him stood and saluted stiffly. She was solidly built and wore a
brocade coat in black and gold that had a stiffness that suggested
armored scales were sewn into it. "And Sheikh Rashid ibn Ahmed,
a Qamarist priest." The man to Ryōma's left stood and offered his
hand. Shono shook it. *Ah, is that where we get the custom from.*
Rashid wore a long white caftan and a neatly trimmed beard.

"A pleasure to meet you, Prince Shono," he said.

"And last, Father Nestor, of the Nasrenes." The man to Ryōma's
right stood and shook Shono's hand as well. He was broad in belly
and shoulder, with a long bushy beard streaked with grey and an
impish twinkle in his eye.

"Don't worry about me," boomed Nestor. "I'm no one important, but the game needs four players, you see."

"I'm not familiar with the Nasrenes," Shono said.

"One of several religious minorities to be found in al-Zawira," said
Ryōma. "I believe it's a tradition that has its roots even farther west."

"Don't get either of these priests started," said Captain Izad.
"Given half a chance, they will talk your ear off about God, or philosophy, or anything else that catches their fancy."

"Guilty!" boomed Nestor.

6. Gods and Wine

Utaku Chiseko,
Who rode with Shinjo long ago,
Told her men they must not drink.
They swore their vows with a wink.

As he left the garden, Shono found Yumino falling into step behind him. She asked no questions and offered no commentary, simply following as he walked the streets of the Inner City. Without a guide to lead them, Shono found the streets simple enough to navigate in their mathematical regularity, but devoid of any strong indication of where to go. Aside from the towering dome of the Grand Temple, each palace in Round City looked much like the last in its uniqueness. For a moment, Shono feared he would lose his way entirely and be unable to locate the Prince's Palace, but turning a corner, he found himself before the whimsical silver tree and regained his bearings.

In the end, he had to ask one of the black-clad guards for directions to Mandana's quarters, which proved to be in a tower built into the wall itself. The guard who directed them made a ward against evil and hurried away once he learned where they were trying to go.

"Stay away from that one, sayid," he said. "Even djinn fear to cross her."

Shono translated for Yumino's benefit as they approached the tower. "You see, Yumino-san. Someone shares your opinion of

Mandana-sama."

"No," she corrected him. "That man fears her. I merely mistrust her. There is a difference, my lord."

Shono thought about that one as they walked through the empty plaza leading up to the wall. *Is that the way of things? I mistrust the caliph, but I do not fear him. Perhaps I should. He could have me killed on a whim.*

Something dragged Shono out of his reverie as he stood before the narrow door to Mandana's tower. The bricks that rose above him were the color of the desert sand, and the silence that hung over the area was as oppressive as the blazing sun high ahead. Shono looked up, and up and up to the top of the tower, where a vulture fluttered its wings and peered down at him.

"My lord?" Yumino asked.

"Do you smell something?" Shono murmured. She shook her head no. He shrugged and knocked on the door. The lengthening silence swallowed up the sound of his knuckles rapping on the sun-warped wood. Shono shifted his weight, casting his senses around the tower, the wall, the plaza surrounding them. He turned away, peering into the shadows cast by the closest palaces, set a bowshot away from the walls. *Something is wrong. It's as if I'm being watched, but no one is there.*

At length, the door opened. Nothing and no one greeted them save the smell.

The smell. *Fortunes, kami, and Lords of Death, the smell.* Shono reeled as the smell slowly unfolded around him. A stink like a charnel house, like old meat left too long in the sun, like rot and corruption, like an infected wound. Yumino wrinkled her nose and dropped a hand to the hilt of her sword.

"My lord?" she murmured.

"I think we'd best see what's inside, don't you?" He stepped through the door.

Within was a broad, undecorated chamber. A large table stood in the center of the room, its surface scarred and splintered and stained a dark, disturbing red. Chains, some ending in hooks, hung from the ceiling of the room. A smaller table stood close at hand, covered with shining metal implements of pain and butchery. A hole, like a well shaft, sat a little off-center in the lowest part of the flagstone floor, obscured by a rusting iron grate.

How many people have died here? How much did they suffer before the end came? The smell was worse here, coming and going in waves, tendrils of stench wrapping around him.

"Who opened the door?" Yumino murmured.

"I did!" boomed a voice, and suddenly a man stood between them. He was tall—head and shoulders taller than Shono—with skin the color of polished lapis lazuli. His bare feet were planted on the stone of the tower floor, and his arms crossed across his bare chest. He wore a Nehiri-style turban, baggy pants, and golden chains around each wrist.

Yumino's hand was on her sword and she had fallen to a fighting stance by the time Shono stopped her with an upraised hand. "I am Shinjo Shono, guest of the caliph," he said, gagging from the stench. "I seek Sheikha Mandana."

"I know who you are, Prince Shono," said the man. *The djinni,* Shono decided. *No human could have surprised me so utterly, could have just appeared in front of me like that.* "You may call me Ma'aruf." He gestured to the stair against the wall. "My mistress is in her chambers, upstairs. I am commanded to escort you thither."

Shono noted the chains at Ma'aruf's wrists. *Commanded? Mistress?* He thought of the statue, the bird perched upon the djinni's hand. "Does not the Prophet forbid slavery, of both humankind and djinn?"

Something sparkled in the djinni's eyes. *Red eyes, like chips of garnet.* "So I have heard, sayid. This way, please."

They climbed quickly upward and through a door set in the ceiling, leaving the djinni behind.

"So," came Mandana's voice of honeyed stone. "You have seen the final fate of those who would defy the caliph and earn my wrath. Are you very shocked? Are you displeased?" Shono did his best to control his gorge. There was no thought left for the dispassionate face of Bushidō; he would consider it a triumph not to vomit all over the stone mosaic floor in this new, much more attractive apartment. "I see that you are. Tell me, my prince. What punishment do you Unicorn have for traitors and thieves?"

A dressing screen, carved with fanciful birds and roaring cats of every description, stood against one wall. Mandana emerged from behind it, wearing a long, loose robe, her bountiful hair piled up atop her head. She tied it in place as he stared, dumbfounded. "Has the cat eaten your tongue?" she asked with a musical laugh. "Ma'aruf, I commanded they be unharmed." The djinni appeared among them and bowed his head.

"Thieves are...branded or exiled," Yumino gasped out from Shono's side. *Mandana is speaking Rokugani*, Shono realized with a start. "It's forbidden to shed Unicorn blood, so traitors are wrapped in a carpet and trampled to death by horses."

"I doubt very much that the traitors care whether they suffer your fate or mine, in the end." Mandana crossed to a table near the wall and poured a red liquor from a crystal decanter. "May I interest you in some wine? I find a glass does a tolerable job of clearing the smell from my nose."

Shono took a ragged breath, looking behind him. A door had fallen shut across the staircase, blocking out the worst of the smell. Already he could breathe again. "Your offer is too kind," he managed. "We cannot accept; we come unannounced and uninvited."

"But not unwelcome," Mandana purred, swallowing a mouthful from her porcelain cup. "You have found me just finishing my bath, but if you will both wait a moment, I can dress properly to receive you." She gestured to a Nehiri-style table and cushions, then vanished behind the dressing screen again. "Ma'aruf, offer them any food or drink within this tower, and tend to them as a servant would."

"As you wish," the djinni said.

"We should leave," whispered Yumino.

"Mandana-sama asked us to wait," chided Shono with more bravery than he felt. *In her own strange way, Mandana has been more honest with me than anyone else in this city. Surely murdering me and my yōjimbō in her apartments is not in her interests.*

They sat, Rokugani style, and looked around the room as Ma'aruf folded his arms, nodded his head, and vanished in an eyeblink. There were exotic carvings in wood and stone adorning the walls, golden lamps burning with smokeless flame, and shelves upon shelves of books and scrolls from every corner of the world. The windows were tall and narrow, as befit a fortification, but the light they admitted reached every corner of the room and made it feel larger than it truly was.

Ma'aruf returned, again simply appearing in the middle of the room, now holding a tray with a Rokugani tea service upon it. Wordlessly, he set cups and poured tea—no proper tea ceremony, but tea nonetheless.

"Quite the comfortable lair for a wicked sorceress, no?" Mandana asked as she emerged from behind her dressing screen once more. She wore a gown of golden silk, with elaborate gold jewelry adorning her otherwise bare, muscular arms. "That is what you believe, is it not?" She sat herself on a cushion between them, smiling her predator's smile. There was no teacup for her.

"It is a…surprising contrast from the room below," Shono said after a time.

"How diplomatic, my prince. Yes, anything would be, I suppose. But that is where the drain is located, and executions can involve quite a bit of blood." She gestured at a door in the wall. "I usually come and go from the wall-walk, as do my guests. A more…picturesque route."

"You are the caliph's executioner, then?" asked Yumino. A good samurai, she did not allow the frown in her voice to touch her face.

"Sometimes. The difference between me and some dullard with an ax is that before a traitor dies, I can learn something worthwhile." She splayed her fingers out on the surface of the table, and for a moment, Shono had the image of a tiger's claws, idly scratching deep grooves in the wood. "Is that why I have been graced with your presence? Have you come to learn?"

"Always, Mandana-sama," Shono choked out. "Saadiyah has shown me that when negotiating, it is best to know not only the issue to be discussed, but also the people with whom one sits and speaks."

"So you come to me to learn more of the caliph? Or of lovely Saadiyah?" Her smile had all the amusement of a cat contemplating a bird.

"I come to learn more of you," Shono said. "Are you not the caliph's most trusted advisor?"

Mandana's laugh was like a waterfall, thundering and beautiful. "So, you saw beneath her veil and found the contempt Saadiyah has for our dear caliph, did you?" She waved a hand to dismiss any protestations Shono might muster and fixed him with a golden stare.

"Saadiyah has her reasons to hate me, and Harun al-Hakim. Yet she is clever and clear-sighted, and the caliph values her advice despite it all. You see, the caliph is a man who knows the value of his tools and has the wisdom to deploy them to their best effect. You see a man who is indolent and oblivious, but in fact, he is an able administrator with the good sense to delegate his day-to-day responsibilities."

The cup of tea sat in front of Shono. The djinni stood behind. *People. Tools. All the same to her, to the caliph she serves.* "Are you one of the caliph's tools?" Shono asked. *Is a samurai a tool? Bushidō gives us all roles to play. Mitsuko was a good samurai, a tool disposed of by her lord. But we Unicorn are not so callous with our people. We wouldn't even treat a horse so callously.*

Mandana's smile didn't waver, but her eyes snapped to him. "The caliph has been good to me. He finds me useful, as I find him."

A strange sort of honesty and honor. Shono held her gaze. *Useful.* "And Ma'aruf. Do you find him useful?"

"Prince Shono, are you objecting to my treatment of my servant?" She snapped her fingers. "Djinni, tell him. Do I mistreat you?"

"No, mistress."

"I merely wonder if you might put golden chains around my wrists, or the wrists of my people, should I misstep," said Shono.

Mandana smirked.

"What will Harun ask of me, Mandana-sama? What is the price of continued peace between the Caliphate and the Unicorn?"

"You must return the lands and peoples conquered by Shinjo Khulan Khan. You must give us the Sand Road."

"The lands and peoples of the Sand Road never belonged to the Caliphate."

"They are Qamarists. That makes them part of the Caliphate."

"Some of them are, and some of them are not. None wish to be fitted for chains."

Mandana spread her fingers before her, as if to ward off Shono's displeasure. "Ma'aruf is not my slave, sayid. He is paying off his debt to me, nothing more. Ask any priest: slavery is forbidden by the Nameless Prophet." She stood and gestured to the door behind them. "Perhaps you would prefer to take the upper exit, along the wall?"

After leaving, they walked along the top of the wall to the closest gate, finding a stair down to the street level there. The guards at the gate made no move to stop them, so Shono and Yumino proceeded to the Middle City and soon found themselves in the midst of a crowded market, where awnings of colored cloth held back the blazing sun, and stacks upon stacks of books and scrolls threatened to spill out into the street at every turn. "The Market of Books," Shono said.

"Look, my lord," said Yumino, plucking a codex with a faded blue cover from the nearest pile. A single Rokugani character, meaning either "love" or the name "Ai," adorned the cover. "A pillow book, and so far from Otosan Uchi?"

The bookseller leaned over the wall of books that separated him from the street and began haranguing Yumino in rapid-fire Nehiri. She replaced the volume, bowed, and backed away.

"Come," Shono said. "I wish to find Sheikh Rashid's temple. It is not far from here."

The temple overlooked the Market of Books just as Rashid had promised. It was only slightly larger than the homes and shops that crowded the streets nearby. Its principle distinguishing feature was a tall spire with a balcony, where several crows lurked, doing their best to stay out of the hot sun. The temple sat at a corner, with doors on both facing streets, and Shono found himself chased away by a fearsome older woman who gasped and veiled her face with her head wrapping when he entered. "What are you doing?" she shrieked. "This entrance is for the women; go around, go around!" Shono apologized and bowed his way out while Yumino stared with a hand on her sword, unsure how to respond. Shono went to the other door, where he was met by a laughing man of perhaps forty years, with a neatly trimmed dark beard on a Nehiri face that seemed well made for laughter and smiles both—Rashid ibn Ahmed.

"Prince Shono," he said. "So good to see you again. Come in, come in. The women's side of the temple is set aside for their privacy; they do not welcome intruders."

"Are you a priest only for the men, then?" Shono asked as he removed his boots in the entryway and followed Rashid through a wide room covered with intricately patterned rugs.

Rashid gestured to the long wall to his right, which Shono saw was more of a screen, its carvings and designs blocking casual vision but not sound. "A prayer leader on either side can preach to the faithful on both sides of the screen. The Word of the Prophet is intended for men and women alike—for all people—both human and djinn."

"You preach to djinn?" Shono thought of Ma'aruf standing in the temple. It seemed impossible.

"I would, if any came when I sang the call to prayer. They are children of God, just as we are, although their role is somewhat different in our world."

As Rashid led him into the garden behind the temple, Shono was silent, thinking back to what Iuchi Shoan and his father, Iuchi Daiyu, had taught him of the history of their *meishōdō* magic. It was learned during the fall of Rempet, he recalled, a century or more before the birth of the Qamari Prophet. He wondered if any Iuchi shugenja had ever read the Word of the Prophet, to see what role the djinn played in the Qamarist idea of the world. *Perhaps I should invite Rashid to return to Rokugan with me; our shugenja could learn much from him.*

Rashid led him to a small game table in the corner of the garden, where a blooming tree warded off the worst of the burning sun. Father Nestor in his dark robe already sat at the table, smoking from a silver pipe. "Rashid," said the big man. "And Prince Shono! What an unexpected delight."

Shono bowed. "You are too kind."

Rashid spread out his cream-colored caftan and sat on a cushion. "Now, Prince Shono, I do not think you came to me to speak of djinn, nor to play *shatranj*. Ask your questions."

"I seek to understand the way of your people," Shono said. "To understand the thinking of your caliph and find a path to peace between the Unicorn Clan and the Nehiri."

"There is your first problem," said Nestor. "I am Nehiri, but you need fear nothing from my quarter. There will be peace between you and me, between all children of God."

"God the Bringer of Peace desires peace on earth between all humankind," said Rashid.

"I fear I do not understand you," Shono said. "Do you each speak of different gods? In Rokugan, we find it helpful to give the

Fortunes names, so that we can tell one from the other."

Rashid smiled and shook his head. "The sorcerers of Rempet used the True Names of humans and djinn alike to command them. To speak a god's name is to invoke them, just as the sorcerers of long ago." He gestured heavenward. "So we will swear by the light of Lord Sun, or beg for the grace of Lady Moon. Yet also we acknowledge that these old deities are but facets of the same God."

"So you have but one god, with many names. It seems quite a chore for a single god to manage the affairs of Heaven."

"Nothing is beyond the power of God the Almighty," said Nestor. "And so you see, there is some question whether we Nasrenes and the Qamarists worship the same God, by different names, or if only one of us worships the true God and the other a false idol."

"By extension, the same debate applies to your religion as well, Prince Shono," said Rashid. "The Word of the Prophet is for all humankind. Including you Rokugani."

Shono bowed slightly, doing his best not to smile. "We have no need for the Word of the Prophet in Rokugan—we have our own. Thanks to Shinsei's wisdom, there is no debate as to which god is true and which is false. Our priests commune with the kami and the ancestors regularly."

"Your religion seems a very practical one," said Rashid, laughing. "No wonder you believe so easily."

"My belief is not required," Shono said. "That the Kami Shinjo founded my clan and led us on our great journey across the Burning Sands is a matter of historical record. That her divine blood runs in my veins, as my ancestor, is likewise not a matter of faith but of fact. The prayers of the shugenja to the kami are answered directly, and none can doubt their efficacy after seeing the miracles they work. We in Rokugan have daily, irrefutable proof of the role of the kami and the Fortunes in the Celestial Order. Even the power of the Ujik Lords of Death is not in dispute."

"Are you a scholar of your Celestial Order, Prince Shono?" Rashid asked, setting aside his own pipe.

"I have read the Tao of Shinsei," Shono said. *Most of it, anyway.* "But I would not call myself a scholar, no."

"I suspect that if you spoke to a scholar of your own religion, you would find that there is considerably more debate and disagreement as to the nature of your Celestial Order than you suppose."

"Perhaps so," Shono allowed. "But we were speaking of your own—ah—faith."

"Quite," said Rashid. "I understand you treat with the caliph. Understand that the caliphs are the inheritors of the authority of the Nameless Prophet. The Prophet was the commander of great armies, the supreme master of a nascent empire that brought peace and order to the Cradle of the World, where only chaos had reigned before."

"Thanks to that Kami Shinjo of whom you are so proud," Nestor interjected. "It was she, and the al-Qamari, who cast down Old Rempet."

"You'll just confuse the boy." Rashid sighed. "The al-Qamari were a secret order opposed to the Sun Kings. They called themselves the Children of the Moon, and they held their meetings and did their acts of rebellion at night, far from the sight of Lord Sun. When the Prophet brought his teachings to the Cradle of the World some two centuries later, his followers took up the name of the al-Qamari to rally around."

"And that is why you call yourselves Qamarists?" Shono asked.

"Yes," allowed Rashid. "And why sometimes you see the silver disc of the moon used as a symbol for our people."

"But not just the Nehiri people. We have Qamarists who owe their fealty to Shinjo Altansarnai Khan, my mother, but most of our people follow the Tao of Shinsei. I must assume that some do both."

"And that is what must be complicating your relationship with the caliph, eh?" Nestor chuckled.

"It isn't a matter for laughter, Father," said Rashid.

"It is when I have no part in it for good or ill. You see," he turned back to Shono, "the Prophet never established a formal priesthood to interpret his Word. It's up to each of his followers to do that for themselves. This man," he slapped Rashid on the shoulder, "that you call 'priest,' would better be called 'teacher.' And yet the great and powerful after the Prophet's death—or disappearance; that's a matter of some debate as well—decided to promote one of their own to take the Prophet's place as the speaker of the Word and the Protector of the Faith."

Rashid sighed. "Almost as soon as he was appointed, the first caliph faced resistance and controversy. The first great schism of the Qamarist faith was between those who rejected the office of the caliph and those who obeyed. Since that time, the caliph has enjoyed more ceremonial and theoretical power than true dominance over the Qamari world."

"And this caliph is the worst of the lot," Nestor said.

"Father!" protested Rashid.

"I'm no Qamarist; I can say it without committing blasphemy," Nestor said, chuckling again. "And you agree with me, or you'd cast me out of your garden directly." He turned to Shono and leaned forward, slapping the table with his palm. "Listen. Harun al-Hakim is a wicked man. He never met a vice he did not enjoy, nor a sin he would not happily commit to gain more wealth and power for himself. And his followers know it. He must resort to hostage taking, blackmail, and the threat of his armies to keep the emirs and sultans of the Cradle of the World and the Sea of Jewels under his thumb." *With the way he drinks and the pleasures he insists on sharing with his allies, I can well believe it.* "The Prophet forbade sorcery, yet the caliph keeps a sorcerer always close at hand. Why, except that she offers him power?" *Mandana.*

"The Prophet forbade the enslavement of djinn," said Rashid. "To read such a law as a ban on sorcery is not a settled thing."

Nestor held up a hand. "I am certain our guest cares little for the nuance of our theological debates. You cannot deny that the caliph's reign has met with less than universal acclaim from the priests throughout the Cradle of the World."

Rashid sighed. "I cannot. Nor do all his emirs and sultans follow his lead with perfect loyalty."

"If the caliph were to achieve some great triumph," Shono conjectured, "such as extending his rule to include Qamarists in foreign lands, might that secure the loyalty of many of those priests and emirs?"

"It might," said Rashid.

"And if the caliph were to suffer some great defeat, such as losing a war with a foreign power, might he contrariwise suffer a general revolt against his tyranny?"

"Hah," laughed Nestor. "The caliph keeps the children of half his emirs hostage in the Round City. Freeing even one of his caged birds could be enough to throw the caliph into a war against his own people."

"Recall, Father Nestor, that even if you proclaim a different faith, you must still bow to the law of the Sultan of al-Zawira." Rashid sighed and stood. "It would pain me to see you dragged to the caliph's dungeons."

Or to Mandana's tender mercies. Shono stood as well, sensing their audience was at an end. "I thank you, Rashid-sensei," he said.

"Sensei?" asked Rashid.

"Ah, it means 'teacher,'" Shono answered.

Nestor barked a laugh. "Hah! What did I tell you?"

"I hope I have given you the guidance you need to find a path to peace, Prince Shono."

"So hope we all," said Shono. He bowed to Nestor as well. "And my thanks to you, too, Nestor-sensei."

As Shono stepped into the street again, soon followed by Yumino through the other door, he saw Rashid appear on the balcony atop the tower overhead. In a high, clear voice, Rashid began to sing, a warbling call that seemed to dance above the rooftops. "God is great!" he sang. "There is no god but God, and we know Him through His Prophet!"

"The call to prayer," said Saadiyah from behind him. Shono turned and bowed. *Am I truly so distracted, to let a courtier sneak up on a Shinjo-trained scout?* "How did you find Sheikh Rashid?"

"He is a wise and amiable man," Shono said. "I was unaware you were familiar with Sheikh Rashid."

"No? There are few teachers in the city who can match his insight into the Word. I favor his temple for prayer and scholarship whenever I can."

"I would not keep you from your prayers," Shono said, bowing.

"Thank you. I hope that your visit was fruitful." Saadiyah bowed her head and walked through the women's door into the temple. The black-clad guard who was her shadow stopped outside the door and assumed the intimidating blankness of guards everywhere.

"You do not pray?" Shono asked the man. He received only an annoyed glare in return.

Shono let his feet lead him as he left the temple. Yumino walked silently two steps behind him, and he thought, and watched, and listened. *By the laws of the Caliphate, it seems the Ganzu belong to them as much as they are Unicorn.* He could see a path forward, redrawing the border at the Hidden Valley, still controlling most of the trade. An adjustment to the tariffs in both directions; details for Ryōma to consider. It would be a stiff loss for the Unicorn, a loss of face for Shono, and a great victory for Harun al-Hakim. But it would prevent a war. *Mitsuko, screaming, sword drawn.*

A small intake of breath from Yumino snapped Shono's attention back to the present. Chagatai swaggered down the street toward them, gazing around himself in frank amazement. *What is he doing here?*

"Cousin," said Shono, falling into step at Chagatai's side. "I had not looked to find you in al-Zawira."

"No?" asked Chagatai. "I would not come all this way and then not see its splendors for myself, Cousin."

"I had not looked to find you in al-Zawira, because I instructed you to guard our camp."

"And guard it I shall," said Chagatai with an easy wave of his hand. "I have a dozen Moto warriors at my command, Shono-san. They are each capable of standing guard for a few hours while the rest of us take our leisure in the city."

"And if misadventure should befall them in the city?"

"Then they are hardly worthy of the claim of being a Moto warrior, are they?" He reached out one hand and clapped Shono on the shoulder, a blow that might have felled a lesser man or a small horse. "Come, Cousin. Let us find what passes for a sake house and get drunk."

The idea of doing as Chagatai was doing, and taking leave of his responsibilities for a few hours, suddenly was very attractive indeed. Shono would rather climb on a horse and ride into the sun and never return, but since that didn't seem to be an option… "Yes," Shono said. "Let us."

Finding a sake house was harder than Shono thought it would be, and he found himself remembering Saadiyah's words that the Prophet warned against the excesses of wine. At length, they settled for buying a few bottles of deep burgundy wine from foreigners in tunics the same color with gold patterns dyed into the hem and sleeves. The strangers spoke no Nehiri that Shono could identify, nor any Rokugani, but they understood the word "wine" well enough, and so they made a merry company, walking the streets of al-Zawira with jugs of wine in hand.

"To foreigners," Chagatai cried, lifting the clay jug in his hand and throwing back a long mouthful of wine. "May they always flout the Prophet's laws to our benefit!" Shono followed suit; he found the taste almost repulsively sweet, but after a few swallows it produced a most agreeable warm feeling in his belly.

"Yumino-san, do not wrinkle your nose at us. Drink!" Chagatai waved his jug in her direction. She took it and sniffed suspiciously, then tried a tentative sip. Chagatai guffawed and drank directly from the bottle, apparently content with this victory.

"How do you find the city, Cousin?" asked Shono after another swallow. "You speak no Nehiri, I think? How do you navigate?"

Chagatai shrugged. "The people are friendly enough, and all half-terrified of the fearsome Unicorn who have twice brought their city to its knees. As for the language, I find that pointing and waving a fistful of coins works as well here as it does in Khanbulak. Half of being welcome anywhere is believing that you should be."

"And the other half is coin?"

"It helps!" Chagatai lifted his bottle. "To money, which flows along the Sand Road and makes our clan the equal of those others with more history and connections to their name."

"A samurai should not concern themself with such mercantile matters," Yumino reminded him.

"No? The Ide certainly do, and we should thank them for it. Only the truly rich can afford to ignore matters of money and trade." He paused in his swagger, pursing his lips at the sight around them. From the trading house where they had purchased the wine, the three samurai had wandered toward the river and now stood in a district of tall warehouses with vaulted roofs, workshops for the construction and maintenance of riverboats, and long, low tea shops and cafés with dying trees in their courtyards. The buildings all had a slightly shabby air, crumbling here and there with weathered and warped doors and shutters, where there were any.

The people lining the street were even more ramshackle. Some had the broad shoulders of laborers, but most were scraps of flesh hanging from bones, with the enormous bellies of starvation. Some had mangled or missing limbs, but others showed no sign of what, if any, misfortune had cast them into their current extremity.

"As you say," said Shono. *Tools with no use. Discarded.*

"Have these people no ordu to care for them?" Chagatai wondered. "Where are their families? What is wrong with this city?"

"There are beggars in Unicorn lands, too, Cousin."

"Not so many, not even in Khanbulak. And not so…desperate." Chagatai grunted and turned his back, leading them away from the river and toward a more prosperous prospect. "If money truly didn't matter, I'd say let the caliph have the Sand Road, let him trade with the Ivory Kingdoms and cut us out. But while our war with the Lion remains unresolved, we cannot afford to give up any of our wealth, power, or influence at court. I'd not see my clan sitting with a big belly on a beggar's blanket."

"So you admit that steel alone is not enough to win a war," Shono mused. "Cousin, you surprise me. The Moto have a reputation for a more simplistic view of conflict."

"Well, I blame your bloody ancestor saddling us with Khanbulak," Chagatai groused. "We've grown civilized these past generations. Clearly, we'd like that feeling to go away as soon as possible."

Shono laughed, and they drank again.

"You are in a better humor than has been your habit these past few weeks," Chagatai observed. "Are the caliph's amusements delightful, then?"

"The caliph's amusements are tedious," Shono admitted. *But I do feel almost…well.* He paused a moment to study the spires of a nearby temple. "But I am a Shinjo. My chief delight in this city has been meeting its people and learning their strange customs and beliefs."

"Some stranger than others," Yumino muttered.

"*Enh?*" asked Chagatai.

"Yumino-san is still unsettled by our meeting with the caliph's pet sorcerer," Shono said.

"Tall woman, glare like an eagle, moves like a hunting cat?" Chagatai asked. "I saw her. 'Strange' is the word."

"Careful, Cousin, you sound almost as if you admire her."

"That woman is not one to admire," Yumino said. "She has no honor, and only false courtesy."

"One sip and our little battle maiden is as chatty as a fat old veteran," chuckled Chagatai. Yumino flushed and looked down at her wine. "Enough of the caliph and his pet sorcerer. Let us drink to absent friends." He poured a mouthful of wine to the dusty street. Each of them raised their drink.

The faces of the fallen swam in Shono's vision: those who had ridden with him in battle and those who had fought against him. *Mitsuko. Taka.* "To absent friends," he said, and drank.

"Tell me true, Shono," said Chagatai. "Is this what you want from your life? Is this what you see as your future as khan, traveling to the court of those who hate you to make compromise after compromise? To watch your clan being worn away like a riverbank—a treaty here, a scrap of paper there?"

"Leave it be, Chagatai-san," groaned Shono. "What will be will be, and I will do my best."

"Just as your mother does," said Chagatai. "She signed her treaty, agreed to her marriage, watched as the Lion gobbled up the best the Unicorn had to offer, stripped our clan of its dignity…and then she said 'no,' and she took up her sword, and stood up for her people!"

"She broke her word," growled Shono. "She dragged her honor—our honor—behind her horse. For her people? Or because she wasn't willing to sacrifice her own happiness for the good of the clan?" *Five winds, how long have I been swallowing that anger?* He staggered, suddenly exhausted. It felt like a dam had burst, like a torrent had flowed out of him and left him empty. He tried to fill the emptiness with another swallow of wine.

"Is that what you think you did?" Chagatai asked.

"What?"

"When you rode to Hisu Mori Toride. Did Altansarnai Khan order you to lead the battle against your betrothed?"

"No," Shono said. "She would have spared me. But the Lion tasked Mitsuko with that first attack for a reason. They wanted me to back down, to look weak. What choice did I have?"

"You could have stayed behind to garrison the castle. You could have led a counterattack elsewhere into Lion lands. You could have reinforced any of the other villages along the border. Instead, you and your pride rode straight into a battle that any Unicorn commander could have handily won." Chagatai leveled a finger at Shono, a lance at his heart. "You made that choice, Shono-san. And it destroyed you."

"Do you think me so weak?" hissed Shono.

"I think you have thought of nothing since I joined your party except riding west and never returning."

Have I been so transparent? "I have done my duty. I will do my duty. I will serve my clan, always. My mother taught me that…by word if not by deed. The clan comes first."

"She is the Khan of Khans!" roared Chagatai. "She *is* the clan!"

"Khans come and go!" shouted Shono. "Someone else could do the job if she stepped aside." *Did she refuse the marriage because she thought I was not up to the challenge? Fortunes, is that why I'm so upset, because I feel like my mother told me I'm not good enough?*

"I'm glad to hear you say it, Cousin!" cheered Chagatai, veering so quickly from rage to delight that Shono felt unhorsed. "Very well, I accept!"

"Forgive me, I lost track," said Yumino, pink faced. "Did Chagatai-san commit treason again?"

"Unclear," Shono admitted. "Best to blame it on the wine and indulge his childish fancies."

"I know I retain my youthful beauty, Shono-kun," Chagatai said, smoothing out his mustache with one finger, "but I believe I have a few years on you." He hauled Shono away from the wall he leaned upon and draped one arm over Shono's shoulders. "But Cousin! I am pleased to see you fighting back. You are in good humor. Is it a woman?"

Shono shook his head, fighting back laughter. *If it's a woman, it's in quite the opposite way you mean, Cousin.*

"A man, then? It's not me, is it?" He slapped Shono on the back. "Alas, my heart is not free at the moment, Shono-kun; ask again when our mission is concluded."

"I'll be sure to keep it in mind," Shono drawled.

It was only later, staggering back to the Round City as the sun pinked the eastern sky, that he found cause to wonder: How had Chagatai been so familiar with the caliph's desires and the state of their negotiations?

7. The Lion and the Unicorn

A Lion met a Unicorn
Underneath the forest's horns.
The Lion spoke uncivil words.
We answered him with sharpened swords!

By the time he reached the gate of the Inner City, Shono was at least partially sober, although the lack of sleep gave everything a glass-edged tint, as if his world might shatter if he moved too swiftly or spoke too loudly. He therefore at first dismissed the sight of Saadiyah atop the wall above the gate.

Upon emerging in the Inner City, however, Shono turned and saw her still silhouetted there against the light of the eastern sky. She was shrouded, as ever, beneath a long gown of light-brown cotton, but by now Shono had the sense of her stance, her walk, her scent. Not knowing why, he climbed the stair to stand beside her. Yumino remained at the foot of the stair.

"Prince Shono," Saadiyah said as he approached. "You are early emerged from your lodgings." She glanced at his coat, his disordered appearance. "Or perhaps late returned from a night of celebration."

"I have been exploring your city," Shono said. "Mostly, I will admit, a wine shop, at the suggestion of my cousin Chagatai-san." He turned his face to the wind, let it blow through his hair. For a moment it felt like the freedom of the Golden Plains. But just a moment.

"Chagatai-san. This must be Moto Chagatai, the famed warrior?"

"Famed mostly by himself," Shono said. "I have never met a more proud or boastful man." *Except perhaps your caliph.*

"There is much more to see in al-Zawira than wine shops," Saadiyah chided. "Just think! The Court of Wisdom lies within sight of these walls, and instead you chose wine." She nodded in the direction of a sprawling palace, at least the size of any of those in the Inner City, with elegant curving domes and columned court-yards, that stood perhaps two li to the south. "The finest scholars in the Caliphate are gathered there to share their knowledge. Did you know, at the command of Caliph Abbas al-Mansour, the scholars of the Court of Wisdom marched into the desert with their tools." Here she held up an intricate instrument of bronze.

"A strange sort of...compass," Shono guessed.

"A type of astrolabe," she corrected. "Though I am not surprised a barbarian such as yourself is unfamiliar with it. Using this, we can measure the height of the stars above the horizon. The scholars of the court carried these, and other tools, and they went out into the desert where it is flat for many mīl around. They took a sight-ing of the North Star, and then they marched perfectly north in a straight line, taking careful measurements all the while. When the North Star had risen precisely one degree in the sky, they marked their progress, then returned to the beginning and did the same to the south. When the North Star had sunk precisely one degree, they again marked their progress. Do you know what they found, *sayid*?"

"I do not," Shono said. "I suppose they discovered some rela-tion between the height of the star and their distance traveled, but I cannot guess what it was."

"Of course you cannot. In both directions, a journey of fifty-six and two-thirds mīl was enough to move one degree beneath the star. From this, the scholars calculated the size of the entire world: forty and a quarter thousand mīl around." Saadiyah sighed and gazed again at the Court of Wisdom. "To know the size of the entire world, merely from observations here in its cradle. That is the wisdom of the court. I would give much to visit."

"But as you yourself say, it is near at hand. Are you truly forbid-den to pass through its gates?"

"Its gates are no barrier to me," Saadiyah allowed. "Yet forbidden from making the journey I am, all the same." She puffed her cheeks and blew out her lips, like a horse whickering its disapproval.

"It seems odd to me that the caliph would trust your counsel, yet not trust you with freedom of the city."

"It is not for the likes of you or me to question the decisions of the caliph," Saadiyah said.

Shono took a breath and cast his senses wide. *There.* Two guards, on the wall with them in the shadow of the gate to the left and the tower to the right. *She daren't speak ill of the caliph in their hearing, I suppose.* "I believe I understand you, my lady." He paused a moment, considering. "I don't believe you've told me anything of your father, Abdul Rahim, or of the Mozedu."

"Mozedu is a city," she said, slipping her astrolabe into a bag and the bag over her shoulder. "It lies across the Sea of Jewels, not far from Lake Bandu-Xosa, and is one of the richest trading ports in all the Caliphate, save only perhaps al-Zawira itself, or Ninua on the Conqueror's Sea." She closed her eyes and leaned against the parapet. Her face…softened. "I can still remember the smell of the sea, the sparkling light of the water in the morning. I remember the hills overlooking the city, where we grow olives and oranges."

"And your father?"

"My father is the emir of Mozedu. He is respected among the Bandar, both the highland tribes and the merchant princes of the coast."

"Little wonder, then, that the caliph is so protective of you. Surely if he allowed any harm to befall you, he would make a powerful enemy."

Saadiyah favored him with a sharp look. "As you say, my prince. I must take my leave and see what duties the caliph has for me today." She bowed and made her way down the stairs. Shono remained a while longer, thinking, before he and Yumino returned to the Prince's Palace.

When they arrived, they found Ryōma sitting at breakfast, already dressed in the Nehiri fashion.

"You have become Nehiri, Ryōma-san," Yumino said. Indeed, Shono had scarce recognized him. *Even his smell has changed.*

"Perhaps we should all adopt the local style of dress? It seems to be the equal of our own for modesty and comfort."

"You should bathe and perhaps sleep an hour, if you can manage it," Ryōma said. "You look as if you have drunk some poor wine seller out of their stock."

"With Chagatai-san's help, we just might have," admitted Shono. He staggered toward his room to follow Ryōma's advice but was pulled up short by the Ide calling his name.

"Shono-sama. What was Chagatai-san doing in the city?" Ryōma had set down his coffee and now slouched, perfectly still in that apparent slumber that meant he was thinking very hard.

"You find that suspicious as well?" Shono asked. "Good. That suggests I'm not being paranoid."

Shono retreated to his room and collapsed, clothed, on his bed. After far too little time, he was awoken to bathe and dress. His dressing-room servants, a trio of women who compensated for his nudity with their own head-to-toe modesty, fussed at him while he considered, and as a token of peace, he ultimately elected to follow Ryōma's lead and dress as much in the Nehiri fashion as he could manage, in a sky-blue caftan embroidered with crawling vines, with a head scarf of white cotton. Only his Ujik-style belt, from which hung his two swords, remained to mark him as a Unicorn. *And my face.*

By the time he was dressed, Saadiyah was seated in the dining room, laughing at some joke of Ryōma's. "You look every inch the prince today," she said, smiling at his costume. "I am commanded to escort you to the Court of Beasts, where his magnificence hopes you will enjoy a bit of sport."

"By all means, Saadiyah-san, lead on."

She bowed precisely and led them through the door. Once her back was turned, Shono filched a handful of olives and figs from the table and, on a sudden impulse, plucked the jeweled bird from its place. He tucked the bird into his caftan and followed, eating what he feared might be his only meal for the day.

The Court of Beasts was past the Silver Garden and near the great wall on the other edge of the Inner City. It had its own tall walls, carved and painted with animals of every description, some of which Shono dismissed as chimerical fancies. The gate though which Saadiyah led him had a rearing horse standing to one side, a snarling lion at the other, and an eagle with wings spread above.

Who is the eagle? Shono wondered. *Does the caliph set himself in that role? A vulture would be more apt, if he hopes to pick over our corpses after the Lion have finished with us.*

Within the walls, the Court of Beasts proved to be a modest collection of buildings arrayed around a large oval area. The trees and flowering plants that Shono had come to expect from Nehiri gardens still served as natural barriers and markers of paths, but all led to the center, where a number of broad pavilions offered shade for the crowd of courtiers, soldiers, and ministers gathered to watch the spectacle in the oval.

As they approached the center, they passed a large bronze cage on their right, which contained a stunted tree and a colorful chorus of dispirited birds. The building to their left proved to contain its own cages, each displaying a different exotic animal.

"The caliph enjoys putting beautiful creatures in cages, it seems," Shono murmured.

"The caliph takes great delight in displaying exotic animals from the far corners of the world."

I'd rather our hawks had flown away in the Burning Sands than languish in a cage like this. Shono took a breath and stilled his face. They were approaching the edge of the oval, and he could see the caliph sitting atop an enormous cushion and laughing at some folly in the ring.

Shono smelled blood, and his fingers twitched toward the hilt of his sword. *No. If the caliph wants you dead, he'll do it quietly, in secret. Like bandits on the road.* Servants swarmed in the oval as Shono and Saadiyah came to rest against the rail. The servants carried baskets of sand, rakes, and other tools of gardeners, which they used to clean away pools of blood. A cart vanished through a gate to the left, with the corpse of a bull sprawled atop it. Shono wondered what had become of the victor of the last contest.

The caliph was only a few strides to his right, and he gestured Shono closer. "Welcome, Shinjo," he said in his wheezing voice. "I understand that you Unicorns are great lovers of beasts, and so I thought to delight you with some of my treasures."

"You are too kind, my lord." Shono's stomach twisted. *People and beasts alike are things to him. I will like what is to come even less than singers and dancing girls.*

"I have a particular treasure that I think you will find especially pleasing," Harun said. He raised one hand, and his rings glinted in the light. "Do you know what it is? I was very lucky to add it to my menagerie, you know; I was half-convinced they were mythical."

"I couldn't guess, my lord."

"It is a unicorn!" chuckled the caliph. "Here she comes now."

The gate at the far side of the great oval swung open, and a creature trotted through as servants and grooms scattered from its path. It was, arguably, a unicorn, with a single horn rising from above its nose and four feet stamping on the sandy ground. But it was as unlike the unicorn of Shono's clan crest as seemed possible, as unlike the stories as he could imagine. It was grey, its skin warty and tough-looking, with three toes on each foot, and it was practically hairless, with no flowing mane or indeed any grace or beauty to its appearance whatsoever.

"You see?" bellowed the caliph, as much for the crowd to hear as for Shono. "Fat, stupid, and ugly. The perfect unicorn in all respects." Shono heard Yumino, ten paces away, stiffen, felt her hand fall to her sword.

Yet it moves swiftly enough, seems strong and proud. And as for stupid, that I think remains to be seen. "My lord is mistaken," Shono said instead. "The true unicorn was a spirit of light, of fire and water, and the savior of my clan on our journey. This is an animal, although an uncommon strange one, I admit."

"Stories have a way of changing in the centuries since they were first told," the caliph said. "Who knows what the Shinjo of ages past thought when they first encountered this majestic beast?" He chuckled again, then raised another hand. "But I did not bring it here merely so we could see it trot in a circle. My prince, I give you…'The Lion and the Unicorn!' We have prepared this spectacle just for you."

Muscular servants stepped forward, grabbing hold of chains laid in the sand of the oval. They pulled, straining and grunting, and hidden doors opened in the ground, one in each of the four directions. From each came a roar or a scream, and from each leapt a tawny-furred lion. They were thin, rangy beasts, half-starved and hungry for blood. The message could not be less subtle: the caliph was well aware of the Unicorn war with the Lion, and what was more, he intended to profit from it. *Well, now we know who was behind the spy Chagatai's aunt uncovered in Khanbulak.*

The crowd roared with the lions as the unicorn stamped and galloped in its circle. The lions stalked, screaming to one another as they took the measure of their prey. *Three lionesses, one male. How appropriate.*

"Thirty dinar on the male to make the kill!" roared the caliph, his high, wheezy voice strengthened by his bloodlust.

"I will take your bet, my lord," said Shono. "I will bet thirty horses against your thirty dinar that the unicorn is the victor."

"Hah!" bellowed the caliph. "You are walking home, then, Shinjo."

"Do you have thirty horses?" asked Saadiyah. Her arms were crossed across her body, and she alternated between looking at the ground and peering at the animals in the arena.

"Not in al-Zawira," Shono admitted. "I suppose I'd better not lose."

With another roar, the first of the lionesses struck. She leapt upon the unicorn's back, her claws scrabbling for purchase on the beast's rough skin. The unicorn bellowed and spun itself around, but the lion clung to it tenaciously.

"First blood to the lion!" shouted someone to Shono's left. *Yes, it had been.* He remembered Yumino arriving to breathlessly report the death of the Battle Maidens' commander at Hisu Mori Toride, Utaku Hisako. *Slain in a duel by Matsu Mitsuko. My betrothed. Herself cut down in battle by my hand.*

Another lioness leapt for the unicorn, but the horned beast thrashed its head into her path, and the lion fell with a yowl. Blood streaked the unicorn's horn and pooled around the fallen lioness. As she struggled to stand, the unicorn trampled her into the sand until she lay still. *That beast must weigh two tons*, Shono marveled.

The crowd howled, some in dismay, others in excitement. The male lion, with a booming roar, finally hurled itself into the fray. It grabbed hold of the unicorn's face and shoulder with each mighty paw and bit into the beast's neck. The unicorn bleated in a high-pitched wail, then surged forward, carrying two lions as if they were dolls. It slammed itself and the male lion into the sturdy rail so hard the wood splintered, then galloped away before veering back and charging again. The lion clung, biting harder, perhaps knowing that its only hope of survival lay in stopping the unicorn's rampage, until the third time the creature slammed it into the rail. There was a terrible crack, and both railing and lion fell to the sandy earth as the unicorn staggered away. Blood ran from its neck, and its sides heaved with the force of its ragged breathing. But it still stood. The lioness on its back kicked ineffectually with her hind legs, growling in frustration.

The third lioness stalked away, looking for her opportunity, but the unicorn chased after her. The lion yowled in fear and leapt up toward the railing, where several of the caliph's guards, including Captain Izad, rushed to shove the beast back into the ring. The unicorn lowered its head, charged, and slammed its horn into the lion's flank, then flung it to the side, and the dying creature hurtled into the crowd of onlookers after all.

"Perhaps you should increase your bet," Saadiyah suggested as the crowd fled the dying lion, and cursing soldiers ran forward to finish it with their spears.

Shono shook his head. "It's a test of endurance now," he said. "The unicorn is losing blood, and all the lioness on its back need do is stay there until it dies."

"Then is all lost?"

"The poor creature is half-starved. She may have no strength left, either."

The crowd seemed to have lost its taste for the amusement as the unicorn shuffled around the arena, its tail spinning, its sides heaving as it grumbled for breath. The lion on his back occasionally cried out, sometimes gnawed at the beast's spine, leaving no appreciable mark on its tough skin. Long minutes passed as the caliph grew increasingly agitated. Mandana, at the caliph's side, stared fixedly at the pair of animals until Saadiyah pulled her attention away with a murmured comment, perhaps about preparing the next spectacle.

By the time the lion fell, gasping, from the unicorn's back, Shono half expected the unicorn to promptly fall to its knees and expire. Instead, the creature found a new surge of energy, which it used to gore, kick, and trample the exhausted lion into a bloody mass.

The caliph shot to his feet and stalked away, most of his courtiers scurrying after.

"Put that monster out of its misery," snarled Mandana, then followed.

Shono forced himself to watch as Captain Izad summoned a dozen archers and they loosed shaft after shaft into the unicorn until it fell to its knees and lay still. The soldiers approached with spears, and one of them nearly died when the unicorn gave one last charge, but finally they knocked it to its side and stabbed it in its soft underbelly.

"What a beast," said Captain Izad. She turned to Shono and pressed a purse into his hands. "I believe the caliph owes you these thirty dinars, Prince Shono."

Shono juggled the heavy purse in his hands, then tossed it back. "Please ensure all these animals receive funerary rites appropriate to warriors of their courage. Whatever you do for your army's horses will be fine."

Izad nodded, and Shono turned away to find Ryōma, Yumino, and Saadiyah waiting for him, the only other people left in the Court of Beasts.

"Saadiyah-san," said Shono. "You may tell Caliph Harun that I enjoyed the entertainment very much. Tell him I suggest that we arrange for a hunt the next time he wishes to visit Unicorn lands, that he might see how we sport with such noble beasts."

Ryōma interjected. "Perhaps we might arrange for the caliph to visit the Hidden Valley, to see one of the splendors of the Burning Sands for himself. The Unicorn welcome visitors to our lands outside of Rokugan proper."

"As you say," said Shono.

"I will tell him, my prince," Saadiyah said.

"I am no prince," Shono said. "I am Shinjo Shono, heir to Shinjo Altansarnai, of the Unicorn Clan. I am a samurai of the Emerald Empire, the Noyan of the Blue Horde, and the future Champion of the Unicorn and daimyō of the Shinjo." He let himself smile, then, and felt it a feral thing. *Perhaps that "unicorn" was a better symbol of my clan than I first believed.* "And you, Saadiyah-san, may call me Shono-san."

"I will tell him, Shono-san," Saadiyah said, and bowed. Then she was gone, and Shono was alone with his yōjimbō and his advisor.

"What now?" Yumino asked.

"Ryōma-san, that message felt fairly direct; do you agree?"

"Yes, Shono-sama. It was a calculated insult and a threat. I am no longer hopeful that we can resolve this matter through negotiation, even if we were willing to surrender the Ganzu."

"Don't look so discouraged, Ryōma-san. It's not your fault that the caliph is a wicked man who never wanted peace."

"Che," Ryōma growled. "Every time the Shinjo draw their swords, it is because the Ide have failed."

"And what of the Moto?" asked Yumino.

"I refuse to take responsibility for the Moto," Ryōma said.

Shono surprised himself by laughing. There was a fire inside him, a warm and comfortable anger that could substitute very well for happiness. "Nor should you, Ryōma-san. I think it is time for you to ride to the camp and share what has transpired here with Shoan-sama and the others. A messenger must be dispatched to Khanbulak."

"It will be done," Ryōma said with a bow.

"Now, Yumino-san, let us find some place comfortable to wait for the caliph's next move."

"Why not leave now?" Yumino asked. "If the caliph has no desire for peace, shouldn't we leave before he takes our heads?"

"The caliph is not the only person in this city with whom we can negotiate."

8. The Silver Garden

Like the hawk who takes to the wing
To see the world spread around her, I sing
Of hidden glens and ancient trees and waterfalls.
The world is large, but we humans are small.

Shono led Yumino back to the Silver Garden to await whatever would come next, while Ryōma went about his mission and the sun climbed down from its zenith toward the horizon.

"Not the Prince's Palace?" Yumino asked.

"I prefer to be outdoors," Shono said. "I cannot currently gallop across the Golden Plains, so this will have to do."

She nodded and occupied herself with a careful survey of every entrance and exit the garden had to offer. Shono stood beneath the silver tree and studied the branches and the bejeweled birds. Their songs were not very similar to those of any birds he well knew, but allowing for artistic interpretation, they sounded very like birds, and the craftsmanship was exquisite. He thought of the little mechanical songbird Saadiyah had given him.

Saadiyah. The caged bird. He thought of Father Nestor's description of the caliph's plight. *The caliph seeks war to prove his strength to his recalcitrant subjects, and he seeks to conquer the Ganzu to prove his virtue to the prayerful. But he can do neither if his power is threatened from within the Caliphate by even one rebel emir.* He reached inside his caftan and touched the jeweled bird where it nestled against his heart.

But then he heard footsteps in the garden as the sun set, and he turned to find Chagatai stepping from between the trees, Yumino at his heels.

"Cousin," said Shono. "Did Ryōma's message already make the camp?"

"No," said Chagatai. "I have been in the city for some hours. What message did Ryōma carry?"

What business could he have had in the city? "A warning, for my mother. I now believe that the caliph was behind the attempt on my life outside Khanbulak. He has always sought war with the Unicorn, from before I arrived in al-Zawira."

"Not so, Cousin," said Chagatai. "I have just come from a most illuminating conversation with the caliph and his pet sorceress." Shono's eyes narrowed. "He offers me peace and friendship for the Unicorn for all time, as well as a ton and a half of gold and other rewards."

"Chagatai—" Yumino growled, her hand drifting to her sword, but Shono silenced her with an upraised hand.

"This is a matter between me and my cousin, Yumino-san. Stay your hand." She nodded and stepped to the side, where she could put herself between them at a moment's notice. "And what is his price?" Shono asked, at length. He felt his fingers itch, willed his hand to stay away from the hilt of his sword.

"I believe you know it. He demands the fealty of the Ganzu and sovereignty over the Hidden Valley. He wants a new treaty that grants him rights of direct trade with the Ivory Kingdoms, rather than being forced to go through us and grant us tariffs."

"Is that all?"

"No," said Chagatai. "He also offers to make me Khan of Khans."

"Che," growled Shono. "You did always say you would kill me yourself if you wanted me dead. So, is that it, then? Have you come to kill me, or to hear my counteroffer?"

"That is what you Shinjo do, is it not? Bargain and cajole, make deals, and then break them?"

I am not my mother. The warm fire of anger in his belly kindled to a roaring furnace. He felt himself harden, like steel. "My counteroffer," he said. He looked up, to where the great silver tree spread its boughs over his head. *A ton and a half of gold. The caliph's limitless gold, against what?* His fingers brushed the hilt of his sword. *Against my steel.* "My offer is this, Chagatai-san: I offer you nothing. You are a samurai of the Unicorn Clan or you are not. I am the heir to the Unicorn. You will be the Moto khan when your father steps aside, and I will not suffer a khan whose loyalty can be *bought.* Raise your sword against me, and I will cut you down. Call your quriltai, and I will defeat you before them. Otherwise, fall in line and remember your honor."

Chagatai stalked forward, reminding Shono of nothing so much as the lions in the oval arena. *But I am a Unicorn.* "That, Shono-sama," Chagatai said, grabbing Shono's hand with his own, "was the correct answer. Perhaps you have the makings of a khan after all."

Shono took his hand from his sword. The fire in his belly flickered, grumbled. *I'm almost disappointed. Honored ancestors, give me an enemy to fight in open battle.*

"Listen closely, Cousin," Chagatai continued. "The caliph didn't send me here to kill you; he has his own killers. I came to warn you. Even now, they surround us."

Shono glanced to Yumino, who stood with sword in hand and poised to kill Chagatai with a single stroke.

"I hear nothing," Shono said. He closed his eyes. The gurgle of water, the trilling of the birds, Yumino's tense breath, Chagatai's heart pounding with excitement. Footsteps on the street outside the garden. "A dozen soldiers, armed and armored. We are surrounded."

As he spoke, the caliph's black-clad guards came rushing into the garden, scimitars and spears in hand. Captain Izad stood in their midst, her face stone. "Prince Shono," she called. "I am commanded to bring you into custody on the charges of treason and wicked sorcery."

"Your charges are nonsense, Captain," said Shono. "I am not the caliph's subject and therefore cannot commit treason against him. And as for sorcery, you'll pardon me if I laugh."

"Nevertheless."

"I take it I am wanted dead or alive?"

"Alive is my preference," said Izad. "But the caliph will be satisfied with your head." She nodded, and her soldiers advanced, spears and scimitars at the ready.

They had been speaking Nehiri, but soldiers with weapons raised was a statement clear enough for both Chagatai and Yumino. "'Make me Khan of Khans,'" Chagatai grumbled as he drew his sword. "This caliph has no honor at all." Yumino glanced at his sword, at Shono's face, and shifted her attention to the soldiers surrounding them.

"If Lord Shono does not make it through this battle, Chagatai-sama, you die, too," she promised.

"There's only a dozen of them," Chagatai scoffed. "If the caliph had known I would be here, he would have sent three times as many."

Taka dying at the way station. "Shono, you ass."

Shono drew his sword, the watered steel rippling like shadow in the gleaming silver light of the tree. *I want to live.* "Less talking," he said. "More killing. Come, you dogs!" he cried. "See how the samurai of Rokugan fight! When you get to whatever hell awaits you, tell them the Unicorn Clan has returned to these lands!"

"Tell them the Lords of Death have come!" bellowed Chagatai.

The soldiers bellowed their own war cry and rushed forward, lunging with their spears or raising their scimitars.

Yumino was the first to strike, silently raising her katana high, then bringing it down and through her opponent's skull in a fatal blow. She danced away, circling her next foe as he roared and rushed forward. Chagatai, too, rushed the oncoming killers, slamming his shoulder into the first of them and sending him sprawling. The Moto's scimitar swung in a deadly arc, and one of the soldiers lost both his hands in a single stroke.

For his part, Shono flowed like water and stepped around the jab of an assassin's spear. With his empty hand he gripped the spear shaft, and with his sword he lopped his assailant's head from his shoulders. The watered-steel blade parted cloth, flesh, bone as if they were paper. Then Shono was air, leaping back as two more of the killers pounced, leaving them to crash into one another in the space he had just vacated. He touched the fire in his belly and raised his sword once more, cutting through both attackers with two quick strokes. As he kicked the bodies away, he heard Chagatai curse.

"Shono-san, remember when I said the caliph should have sent three times as many warriors?" Chagatai pointed to where another group of soldiers approached, stringing bows. "Killing the caliph's entire army will take all night!" Chagatai complained as he beat back another foe, only to find himself confronted by Captain Izad. The stocky Moto snarled and lashed out, but the Nehiri captain caught his scimitar on her shield, and only Chagatai's surprising quickness saved him from the whistling arc of her cudgel.

"No need to kill them," Shono called. "Only to escape." He lifted the spear he had taken from his earlier opponent and hurled it into Captain Izad's shoulder, driving her to her knees. "Captain, please tell the caliph that we decline his hospitality."

He ducked under another attacker's slash, scraped his sword along the woman's shield, then jumped back as Yumino's blade burst from the guard's throat. Chagatai reached his side a moment later, bleeding from a wound on his arm. The three of them ducked around the silver tree, putting it between them and the archers.

"Right," Shono said. "Yumino, it's time you went and fetched your strongest weapon. We'll all need horses to get out of here alive. Chagatai, get to the Dead City; keep every other there safe. The caliph will be trying to kill us all at once, I think."

"And you, Shono-sama?" Yumino asked.

"I have an important new alliance to make," he said. He pulled the jeweled bird from his caftan and tossed it to Yumino.

She tucked it into her kimono without a word, her mouth a tight line. *She wants to argue, but battlefield discipline is the only thing the Battle Maidens value more than their sacred steeds.* "Hai," she said. "Kiso and I will find you when I have the horses." She ran from the garden so fast she may as well have already been on horseback.

"Good hunting, Cousin," said Chagatai. They clasped hands once more, then Chagatai rushed forward, cutting down the closest guard with a whoop. "Ha ha! Chase me, you gaijin dogs, or are you afraid?" He ducked behind a tree as an arrow hissed past where he had been standing, still booming challenges and increasingly crude insults in Rokugani.

Then Shono was alone, save for the oncoming guards and a wounded Captain Izad. He let them corner him against the garden's wall, then climbed up and over it as nimble as a mountain goat. *Follow if you can.* Dropping to the avenue on the far side, he jogged into the shadows of the next garden in line.

The streets were deserted in the silver darkness of the full moon. Shono made his way toward the Court of Beasts. *I should have bothered to discover where she makes her lodging. Perhaps I can catch her scent where I last saw her, follow her that way.* He saw no servants, no passersby he could interrogate. Except—there. Someone stood in the darkness before him, a deep blue fading into the shadows.

No heartbeat. No scent. "Ma'aruf," Shono hissed.

"God's blessings upon you, Prince Shono," Ma'aruf said, striding forward. "I am commanded to deliver you to my mistress."

"I would rather not kill you, djinni."

Ma'aruf laughed. "I feel the same way, my friend." He vanished and appeared again behind Shono. Shono raised his sword—*too slow*—and Ma'aruf's arm came down like a falling mountain on his head.

9. The Night of Ghuls

Around me spreads a golden sea.

A more bountiful land I'll never see.

As far as I ride and wherever I roam,

The Golden Plains are always my home.

Shono awoke to the smell: the rotten, choking smell, as if a *nerge* hunt had finished directly atop an open mass grave. When he managed to peel his eyes open, he was unsurprised to find himself lying flat on his back on the table in the center of Mandana's chamber of blood. He tested his wrists, his ankles, and found them all bound tightly. *But I am not dead yet, so she must want something from me.*

He turned his head and found Ma'aruf standing as still as a statue in the gloom, garnet eyes glittering. In an instant, Ma'aruf was at his side, dabbing carefully at a cut on Shono's arm. *When did I get that? During the battle? Or after?*

"Fetch your mistress," Shono said on his second try, his throat broken and torn like the Burning Sands themselves. "Let's get this over with."

"No need to fetch me." Her voice filled the room. It came from nowhere, from everywhere, from the shadows. Shono had the briefest impression of something huge, awful, a demon from his nightmares, but then Mandana herself stepped into his vision, smirking. "Welcome to my home, my prince."

"Spare me your courtesies, sorceress. They ring hollow while I am tied to your butcher's block." *What are you doing, you fool? If you are going to survive this, keep a gentler tongue in your head.* Shono struggled to rein in his anger, but it was running wild, an unbroken stallion. *Have a care it doesn't buck you off.*

"Courtesy," Mandana said in Rokugani. "That is one of the tenets of your Bushidō, is it not?"

"It is," Shono said. "And as it happens, attacking guests and locking them in charnel houses is a grave lapse of honor."

"I have never found a code of honor or justice that was not broken more often than it was followed," Mandana mused. She crossed to the table at the edge of the room and examined each of the sinister instruments there in turn, then paused to consult a thick book bound in pale leather. "Even your own mother dishonored herself, did she not?"

This is how it will be, even if I survive the night. Everywhere I go, my honor is sullied by what my mother did. "She made her choice," Shono said. *Yet not all join Mandana in condemning my mother's decision.* "Had she made a different one, you would find fault with that, I am certain, saying that she dishonors herself and my clan by allowing herself to be reduced to a mere daimyō's wife." He turned his head away, and his gaze fell upon Ma'aruf again. "We Unicorn value freedom as much as honor."

"Freedom? That is not Bushidō," Mandana said. "Or have I been misinformed?"

"A samurai lives for others. Protects others. Shows compassion to others. We find that compassion in celebrating our freedom."

"Fascinating. It really is as unworkable and nonsensical a creed as the Word of the Prophet, open to whatever interpretations and justifications the mortal mind can devise." She crossed to the table and leaned over him, grinning down into his face. Her hair fell loose, brushing against his cheek, and the smell of wet blood came with her. Shono surged against his bonds, lunging forward to kick her, bite her, anything, but only elicited a dry chuckle. "The things people do, the lies they tell themselves, all to hide the truth that they cannot face: power over others is everything."

"Power over self is paramount," Shono snarled. *Shinsei said that. I think.*

"Oh, poor deluded prince. If you had any power over yourself, you would stop me from doing this." With casual, effortless suddenness, Mandana reached out with two talon-like fingers and plucked Shono's left eye from its socket. His vision forked, swam, turned in on itself, and then exploded in red-hot pain and blood. He heard screaming and realized in some detached, still-reasoning part of himself that it was his own. When his vision cleared, it was blurred and strange, false feeling as though he were still drunk. But he saw clearly enough to watch Mandana pop his eye into her mouth like an olive, chewing and swallowing with evident relish. He felt himself fall down into the table, into his own head, his vision narrowing as if peering through a long tunnel, his hearing awash with his own heartbeat. *Don't black out. She's distracted. Do something.*

"Why?" he croaked.

"When we negotiate with your mother, sell you back to her, you'll be my creature. I will see through your eyes—eye, I suppose. Your mind, your soul, will belong to me. This is just the first step."

"I'll die, first."

"Only if I permit it. And I do not permit it." She returned to her book, studying its pages. "That is all for today, I think. If we press the issue too quickly, you might get your wish, and we can't have that." She moved away, on his blind side. *I have a blind side.* Footsteps on the stairs, the creak of the door. Her voice filled the room, salt and furnace thunder. "Ma'aruf. Make our guest...comfortable." He heard her smirk, and then the door closed again.

Ma'aruf appeared at his side. "My mistress calls you our guest, sayid. But if you were truly our guest, and so due proper hospitality, you would have called God's blessing upon this house."

"Ma'aruf." Shono felt his mouth moving, felt words spilling out, but he was standing outside again, watching it happen. "Ma'aruf, why do you serve such a monster? Surely she does not deserve the loyalty you show her. Help me."

"It is not a matter of loyalty." The djinni shook his head. "Ifrits such as I are bound body and soul by our word and bargains. I must obey the particulars of my mistress's commands. I cannot simply set you free. But...she has named you as her guest." He leaned forward, his garnet eyes glimmering. "Perhaps she was speaking poetically. For if you were truly our guest, and protected by guest right, you would have called God's blessing upon this house."

His vision swimming, Shono slumped against the table. "I see," he said. *How might Rashid put it?* "May God the Bringer of Peace bless this house."

"Another of the names of God might have been better chosen, but I thank you all the same, sayid." Ma'aruf bowed and began working at the ropes that bound Shono's wrists with fingers as powerful and unyielding as stone. "These ropes are clearly too tight. You must be uncomfortable."

"Thank you," Shono gasped. He turned his head to watch Ma'aruf work, and his head exploded in fresh pain. *She ate my eye.*

"Would our guest like any refreshment? Perhaps a beverage or delicacy that would be difficult or impossible to acquire here in the city?" Shono gaped at the djinni, who sighed theatrically. "The Prophet commands us to offer our guest the finest refreshments that are within our power, and my powers are prodigious."

"*Airag*," Shono said. *He is...helping me.* "Fermented mare's milk. Only brewed in Ujik and Unicorn lands. If you please."

"An excellent choice, sayid. Why, I believe it will take me the better part of an hour to locate such a drink and return."

"Why are you doing this?" Shono flexed the fingers on his left hand, felt blood returning to them. *He was right; I am much more comfortable with the ropes loosened.*

"It is an uncommon prince who takes notice of a lowly servant." With that, the djinni crossed his arms, nodded his head, and vanished.

One hour. I wonder if he meant a Rokugani hour, or a Nehiri hour? It didn't matter. Shono twisted, grunted, felt his skin chafing and tearing beneath the ropes, strained his whole body. He tried to cast out his senses in the Shinjo way, to locate Mandana in the tower above him, but the pain of his eye and his wrists kept snapping him back to himself. It was impossible to concentrate. *It doesn't matter. Either she discovers me while I work to escape, or she doesn't.*

He freed one hand, then the other, then sat up on his third try to pick at the ropes binding his feet. Minutes passed, his blood pounding in his ears. Finally the ropes came away, and he staggered to his feet, leaning on the table as a wave of dizziness attacked him. *The whole world looks wrong. I can't tell how far away anything is.*

He stumbled across the room, avoiding the iron-gated well in the center, and braced himself against Mandana's table. An oil lamp, vials and flasks of oil and who knows what else. The insidious book. Implements of torture, gleaming in the lamplight. Shono watched from outside his body as he grabbed hold of these last and hurled them to the floor with a strangled cry. *She* ate *my* eye.

Gasping, he crawled down the table to the end. His belt with its gold medallions rested there, swords still attached. He grabbed hold of his sword's hilt. He would draw the watered-steel blade, climb the stairs, and kill Mandana. *Don't be a fool. You couldn't kill a half-drowned rabbit right now. You need to escape, find Saadiyah, and complete your mission.*

"Shono!"

"My lord!"

That was easier than I thought it would be. Yumino stood in the doorway, sword in hand and Saadiyah behind her. The samurai stalked into the room like a hunting cat, but Saadiyah simply rushed to his side.

"Your face," she said.

"I will live."

"Not if it gets infected. Hold still, Shinjo, you're not going anywhere like that." One delicate hand splayed open against his chest, holding him in place while the other stroked his face. "Tell your bodyguard to stay alert, please; I will need some few moments."

"I might as well remind her to breathe." Even so, he translated Saadiyah's request.

"Hai."

"You two don't share a language," Shono said while the gaijin selected a bottle from Mandana's array. "How did you find each other?"

"She showed off the jeweled bird I gave you until someone pointed her at me. Then she said 'Shono' enough times that I got the general idea. It was no great leap to suppose that you'd gotten yourself into some trouble. This will hurt."

"Everything hurts," Shono said, but when she twisted his head back and poured a stinging, ice-cold pool of fire into his missing eye, it was all he could do not to scream. By the time he could breathe again, she was pressing folded cotton into his face and wrapping a length of cloth around it. "My lady," he gasped, "I had planned to rescue you from the caliph's captivity, but I see that I got it the wrong way around."

"It's only to be expected from a barbarian."

"Still, I think it best if we flee the city together."

"Yes, let's."

"Shono-sama," Yumino hissed.

Mandana stood in the doorway, blocking their exit to the street beyond. "Somehow you have disposed of my djinni and called your allies to you. I congratulate you, Prince Shono. Few manage even this much of a fruitless and doomed escape." Her voice thrummed through the air like the promise of gathering thunder. With each word she seemed to swell with power.

"Kill her," Shono said in Rokugani, and Yumino leapt forward with a soundless scream. Her sword glimmered in the lamplight but cut only shadow and smoke. Mandana had vanished. "To the horses," he said, but the door slammed shut.

"You fools have no idea of the extent of my powers." Mandana's voice prowled in the shadows, stalking on tiger's feet. Shono shifted, his sword in his hand, straining to find her.

"You do not frighten me, sorceress," said Saadiyah. She busied herself at Mandana's tool bench, her back to the room and showing no care.

"Do you think your precious learning and your benevolent god will protect you from me?" Mandana chuckled. "Will you conjure him down from Heaven like the sorcerers of old?"

"To conjure by the name of God is akin to Name Magic, which is forbidden," Saadiyah said with infinite patience, as if returning to an old argument. "God the Most Bountiful has already supplied his children with everything they need. There is no need to resort to sorcery."

"And what tool has your god provided you with against me?" growled Mandana.

"Bandages, a jar of lamp oil, and an open flame," Saadiyah said. "Shinjo, where?"

"There!" He heard, felt, Mandana gathering herself to pounce, and he pointed. Saadiyah spun and hurled a bottle, its mouth stuffed with burning cotton. It struck the stone floor of the chamber and spread a lake of dancing flame, which revealed Mandana, stagger-ing and shrieking.

Yumino stepped forward and cut, sending black blood streak-ing against the far wall. Mandana howled and faded into the smoke, until only the howl remained.

"Is she dead?" Yumino asked.

"Doubtful," Shono said. He crossed to the door and hauled it open. "But I'll not stay to find out."

"What is that noise?" asked Saadiyah.

Shono paused, focusing his senses. Mandana's final howl wasn't lingering—it was being answered. From down below. *Down the well.* Ten thousand screams, from ten thousand ruined throats, and drawing closer. "We should leave."

Saadiyah nodded, scooped up Mandana's pale book, and fol-lowed the samurai out the door.

Outside, Kiso and Umeboshi were waiting, restless but loyal. Yumino vaulted easily into her saddle, then kept a vigilant eye out as Shono clambered atop his own horse.

"What now?" Yumino asked. Shono made to answer, then saw that she was looking at Saadiyah.

And now those two are best friends. Of course they are. Shono offered a hand and pulled Saadiyah up behind him. "We must leave the city at once, my lady," he said. "Any suggestions?"

"Rashid's temple," Saadiyah called, pointing, and they were off, every hoofbeat a knife of fire through Shono's head.

The gate dividing the Inner City from the Middle City stood open, to Shono's surprise—until he saw the corpses of the guards still lying across the paving stones. "Your handiwork?" he asked Yumino.

"Saadiyah is the one who convinced them to open the gate," she said. "I like her. You chose well."

Chose what? But then they were at Rashid's temple, and Saadi-yah slid off Boshi's back and raced to the doorway.

"Sheikh Rashid," she called softly.

The priest emerged and stared. After a moment, he sighed. "Saadiyah, horses were not part of the plan."

"I know," Saadiyah apologized. "You'll have to bring them

around to meet us. Everyone will be looking for the three of us; no one will think to stop you with our horses."

"Or we leave the beasts here."

"Not an option," said Shono, with a glance at Yumino. *But why can't they simply come with us? What is this plan?*

"We'll need them when we reach the other side," Saadiyah said. "This is nearly two weeks early; the boat isn't ready."

"May God the Shepherd look over us." Rashid sighed. "Yes, of course."

Shono relayed the important points in Rokugani as he and Yumino dismounted. Shono reached for the bow that Yumino had thoughtfully placed in its case on his saddle, but a throb of pain surged from his missing eye. He cringed, lifted the weapon and the quiver, and handed both to Yumino. She took them with a wordless nod.

Rashid took both horses by the reins and vanished down the street. Saadiyah led them into the temple. *Through the men's entrance. I suppose to hell with propriety tonight.*

Perhaps sensing his surprise, Saadiyah called over her shoulder. "God will forgive us, I hope, for using his temple so callously. But if nothing else, we will need Rashid's lamp to go any farther." She plucked a small bronze-and-glass oil lantern from a low table, where Rashid had left it alongside an opened book, then led them into the garden—the same garden where Shono, Rashid, and Nestor had passed that agreeable hour in conversation. She led them to the shatranj board and gestured to it. Yumino stepped forward, grabbed hold, and shoved the thing aside, revealing a narrow passage and a crude wooden ladder.

Shono stared with his one remaining eye. "Did you know about this?" he asked in Rokugani.

"No," said Yumino. She brushed off her hands and began climbing down the ladder.

"She speaks not a word of Rokugani; how is it that she is better at giving you orders than I am?"

Saadiyah climbed down next, holding the lamp. Shono stopped on the second step down, grabbed hold of the game board, and found that it was cunningly arranged on tracks. He was able to close the entrance up behind them quite easily.

"How long have you been planning this escape?" he wondered aloud.

"Four years," said Saadiyah. "When I turned sixteen, I vowed to escape and free my father to act against the caliph's tyranny, or to die in the attempt and free my father to act against the caliph's tyranny."

"A decision worthy of a samurai," Shono said as they crept down the narrow, cramped tunnel. "Where does this tunnel emerge?"

"If the calculations I performed this morning on the wall are correct, in a temple outside the Pilgrim's Court."

An astrolabe can be used to measure distances. "I see," said Shono. "How often are you wrong?"

"I thought you were an idiot barbarian when we first met," she said. "So, never."

It took nearly a quarter of an hour to reach the end of the tunnel. When they did, Saadiyah pointed to the digging axe leaning against the tunnel wall, then at the ceiling. Yumino understood instantly and swiftly cut through the last few finger widths of sandy earth, finding a smooth, straight-edged stone beyond. Yumino kept digging and cutting, and the entire square flooring tile was soon revealed.

"Ah," sighed Saadiyah. "Another ladder or short stair here would have been a clever idea."

"We'll make do," Shono said, stepping forward and making a stirrup of his hands. Yumino stepped up, braced herself against the stone, and pushed. With a terrible scrape, the stone came free, and she hauled herself up into the space above. "You next, my lady," Shono said, and Saadiyah stepped into his hands as well. Shono lifted, Yumino pulled from above, and Saadiyah was soon through the hole, too. Shono's own jump nearly made him black out again, the throbbing in his eye socket was so bad, but between them, the women managed to drag him up to lie, gasping, on the intricately beautiful floor of the temple.

"Now we see if Rashid has made it," Saadiyah whispered. She pointed to the empty hole, and Yumino wordlessly replaced the tile, then brushed away the dirt and grime that marked where they had come through. Saadiyah paced to the doorway, where a sliver of silver moonlight spilled across the floor. "He's not here," she whispered.

The three of them emerged from the temple to find the city streets utterly deserted. "Something is wrong," Saadiyah said. "The Pilgrim's Court should have some visitors, even at this time of night."

A sickly howl echoed across the rooftops. *Just like the voices from Mandana's well.* "Demons walk the streets tonight," Shono said. "We should be glad innocent people have enough sense to shut their doors."

He'd spoken in Nehiri, but Yumino at least understood his tone and his expression. "We must find Kiso," she said. "And the priest."

"Give me a moment," Shono said in Rokugani. The square in which they stood was a large one, flagged in white stone that shone in the moonlight, surrounded by temples and other buildings whose purpose might be visible by daylight but were a mystery now. One such building had a low, flat roof and a stunted cedar tree giving it some shade. Shono jogged to it, handed his swords to Yumino for safekeeping, and began to climb. Every movement sent his vision swimming and his entire body throbbing with pain, but eventually he gained the roof.

Once there, he cast his senses wide, as his sensei had taught him. There were a handful of schools in Rokugan that taught perception and the art of seeing truly. The Kitsuki Method was justly famous—the Hiruma scouts had no equal in the Shadowlands—but Shono still believed that the Shinjo school exceeded them all. *Time to prove it, Shono. How hard can finding two terrified horses be in this city?* He closed his eyes—his eye—and listened, hearing the hissing, screeching, howling progress of the monsters, feeling the sound warp and echo as it passed through the city. And then—there! A scream, and a muffled curse—Rashid was not equal to the challenge of two spirited Unicorn steeds, it seemed.

"This way," Shono called. Yumino tossed up his swords, and Shono snatched them from the air at a run.

With Yumino racing along the street below, Shono leapt from building to building, until he slid down an arched dome and landed on a roof overlooking a place where two streets met. Rashid was still struggling with both horses' reins, and the hissing howl was closer than ever.

"Rashid-sensei!" Shono shouted. "Let them go and run for your life!"

Rashid looked up to where Shono stood. For a moment nothing moved; then a piece of shadow dropped from a rooftop across the way and loped toward Rashid. The priest dropped the reins, and Kiso and Umeboshi both bolted down the street toward Yumino. Shono drew his sword, the watered-steel blade cutting through the moonlight, and leapt from the rooftop with a shout. He hit the ground running and managed to get to Rashid just as the thing grabbed him and drove him to the cobblestones.

The thing had the shape of a man, with ragged black clothing and a scrap of cloth wrapped around its face. In bad light, when it wasn't moving, it might have looked like just another masked killer, right down to the sword at its belt. But its eyes glimmered gold in the moonlight, and its filthy nails were as long and sharp as claws, the skin of its hands a putrid off-white. Shono cut it across the chest and sent it sprawling. The blow would have killed a human being, but the thing stood up and *hissed*, scrabbling for its own sword. Shono swung again, cutting through its neck and sending its head bouncing across the cobbles and into the dark. The body fell like a marionette with its strings cut. Three more of the things dropped down from rooftops, eyes shining in the moonlight.

"Sensei, can you stand?" Shono asked.

Yumino arrived astride Kiso, Shono's bow in her hands. She loosed an arrow, and another, while Shono helped Rashid to his feet. The priest was clutching a wound on his arm where the monster's teeth or talons had found their mark. "A *ghul*," he gasped. "Evil sorcery. A demon bound in the corpse of a human."

"How do I kill it?"

"Remove the head, pierce the heart, or burn it with cleansing flame." Shono translated for Yumino while he helped Rashid onto Kiso's back.

She slipped the bow back into its case. "I'm not the archer you are, Shono-sama. I'll focus on cutting their heads off." She drew her sword, wheeled Kiso as if by a thought, and cut down the first ghul that leapt for her.

"Better to run than to fight, Yumino-san," Shono said. "Make for the river. The Bridge of Boats."

"Hai," she said, and she galloped away.

Shono whistled and found Umeboshi trotting toward him,

Saadiyah already in the saddle with her skirts bunched up around her legs. "You ride, Saadiyah-san?"

"My father taught me to sail and my mother taught me to ride, but I haven't done either in years." She awkwardly pulled herself back to perch on the rear horn of his tall Shinjo-style saddle, and Shono mounted gingerly.

"Some skills, once learned, are never lost. Let's hope riding is one of them."

He turned Umeboshi in a tight circle, then kicked his heels into the horse's flank. "Ya!" The three of them surged forward, following in Yumino, Kiso, and Rashid's wake.

Hooves clattering on cobbled streets, they dashed through the night-clad city. Houses and shops, temples and manors streaked past, their shutters closed and lights doused. It seemed a different city from the one Shono had ridden through only a few days before, as empty as a graveyard. *And as full of death.*

They twice more met with ghuls as they rode. A group of three stood hissing and sniffing where two streets met, and Shono and Yumino rode them down without a pause, swords flickering in the moonlight. Boshi shied away from the monsters, but Kiso rode on unperturbed.

The next group of ghuls leapt rooftop to rooftop, their hissing giving way to the howling of desert jackals. Some of them had weapons in their twisted dead hands, and one or two even loosed arrows in the riders' direction.

"Shono-sama!" Yumino called, racing ahead of him. "The demons are keeping pace!"

It was so. Fast and agile as they clearly were, the monsters would never be able to catch a Unicorn on horseback…unless that Unicorn was burdened with an extra rider. Slowed by the weight of Rashid and Saadiyah, their horses were not pulling away from the hunting ghuls. *Had I two eyes, I might use my bow, pierce their hearts as we ride. But at my best, I might have scored one hit in five when aiming for the heart, and I am not at my best.*

"Ride on," he called forward. "Once we rejoin the others, perhaps Iuchi Shoan will have a solution for our problem." They rode on. Blood pounded in Shono's ears with the hoofbeats pounding on the street. He felt fresh blood on his cheek and realized his eye socket was bleeding again. Shono stood in his stirrups, urging Umeboshi on with each heartbeat, with each sway of his saddle. Saadiyah clung to him, rocking back and forth and silent with her own thoughts, her own fears. *A samurai does not feel fear, no more than he does grief.*

After an eternity, the Bridge of Boats came into view. But no sooner did they approach than Yumino reined Kiso into a tight, clattering circle. "My lord!" she called. "Look."

The crews of the barges that made up the bridge were scurrying back and forth across their decks, pulling ropes and untying each barge from its neighbors. Already the bridge was beginning to pull apart. Saadiyah leaned to see past his back and gasped. "We are too late," she said.

Shono did not pause but spurred Umeboshi on to still-greater exertion. "Shinjo!" Saadiyah called. "You must be either mad or the finest horseman alive to attempt this!"

"I am a Unicorn," Shono breathed, and then they were clattering across the deck of the first boat.

The second boat was a few feet off true, but there was still no water visible between the two boats' hulls, so Boshi took the gap at a brisk trot. Hoofbeats behind announced that Yumino was following, and an arrow striking the deck ahead announced that their pursuers had switched their tactics.

Good. At least they won't be rash enough to follow us. With a wordless shout, Shono urged his horse on to the third boat, then across a widening gap to the fourth. The fifth and sixth had become fouled together, and Umeboshi crossed them at a canter as an arrow shattered the lantern hanging at a barge's stern and spread flame across the deck. Umeboshi shied, but Shono kept his seat and Saadiyah clung even tighter.

The seventh boat was already pulling free with enough water between it and the previous barge that Shono could have lain down in the gap. Umeboshi took the leap as Saadiyah screamed on his back, and for a moment they flew. *Every hope we have for success comes down to whether my horse is strong and fast enough.* Then they landed on the other side and kept on, crossing the eighth and ninth.

Saadiyah's scream of fear became a whoop of delight, then a cry of alarm as an arrow embedded itself in the wood of Shono's saddle. "That was lucky," Shono called, as more fire spread ahead of them.

"Will your horse ride into fire?"

"He will if I tell him to," Shono said, and dug his heels in.

They jumped to the tenth boat, clear over the pool of flame, and the arrows were now falling behind them. They ran across the tenth to the eleventh boat, jumped to the twelfth, and then splashed into the water only a few paces from the shore and hauled out of the river.

"We made it!" exulted Saadiyah. "We're alive!"

Kiso climbed the bank just downriver, Yumino still sitting tall in her saddle. Rashid was slumped over the back of the horse, his white robes stained red where an arrow had pierced his shoulder.

"Rashid!" Saadiyah cried. She slipped off Umeboshi and rushed to the priest's side.

Shono turned and studied the far shore. The river was now a confusion of boats, several on fire, with no evidence there had ever been a bridge. Dark figures, hunched and loping like animals, ran back and forth on the far bank, but none seemed willing to brave the river. "They don't like water?" Shono wondered.

"Thank the kami for small favors," Yumino muttered. "We're out of bowshot, too."

Shono turned his attention to their charges. "Rashid?" he asked.

"He'll live, I think," said Saadiyah. "If we can get him down off this horse and give him some medical attention."

"We can't stop here," Yumino said. "The Dead City is only minutes away."

"Do what you can for him, Saadiyah-san. Then get back on the horse."

"I'm not a physician," Saadiyah complained, but she tore a strip of cloth from her underskirt and fashioned a bandage from it, wrapping it tightly around Rashid's wound with Yumino's assistance.

"Che," Yumino muttered. "We'll need to purify ourselves after this."

But then it was done, and Shono hauled Saadiyah up onto his horse and they rode for the Dead City.

"We're riding *to* the Dead City?" Saadiyah shouted as they approached. "That place is cursed, they say! We should be riding in the opposite direction!"

"That's where my people are," Shono called back. "I'm surprised to find you superstitious, my lady."

"We have been pursued most of the night by monsters out of a children's story. Some small amount of superstition is not just rational, but wise."

"No time for wisdom now," Shono called. He drew his sword. "The ghuls are here, too."

The sounds of battle greeted them as they approached the Dead City, and ghuls swarmed at the edges of the encampment. Hissing and howling as they hurled themselves at the Unicorn, they were naked or draped in rags and burial shrouds, their flesh pale and bloated where it wasn't bruised or green. Their mouths were ragged wet holes, marked by the occasional shine of white teeth and the writhing of long, wormlike tongues. Their eyes were pale in the moonlight, shimmering like an animal's at the edge of the firelight.

The remaining Unicorn were hard-pressed. Most were on foot, and a trail of corpses showed where they had fought a retreat through the crumbling city gates to their current position at the summit of the winged sun statue carved into the rocky outcropping overlooking their camp. A ragged band of surviving ashigaru, led by Bokudō Naosuke, held the line against an endless tide of ghuls, while behind them Ide Ryōma handed arrows to a pair of Moto archers and Iuchi Shoan tended to a wounded Moto Chagatai. The horses and camels in the paddock at the edge of the ruined city, although in a panic of screaming and braying at the smell of the ghuls, at least were unharmed.

"What now?" Yumino asked. Her eyes flicked from the melee, to the paddock, to Shono, and back again. *As my yōjimbō, she feels obligated to grab the horses and run. As a battle maiden, she cannot abandon our companions to their fate. I am not the only one who can feel torn in two.*

Shono drew his sword. "Saadiyah, Rashid. Dismount, please." The anger was back, a warm fire in the pit of his belly. *These are my people Mandana is killing.*

Saadiyah slipped off Boshi, then helped Rashid down from Kiso. "What are you going to do, Shinjo?"

"My auntie there is a sorcerer." Shono indicated Shoan with

a nod of his head. "I'll tell her what Rashid told me about these beasts, and we'll see if she can find a solution. If not, we cut our way to the horses, and everyone who can mount rides east as fast as they can, and everyone who can't dies."

"Take this," Saadiyah said. She pressed the sinister volume from Mandana's lair into his hands. "It might help. May God the Defender of Justice protect you."

"And you," Shono said, then turned Boshi in a tight circle. "We get this book to Shoan," he said in Rokugani. Yumino nodded. "Ya!"

They rode forward, trampling over or threading between the first few ghuls as it suited them. As they reached the denser pack of ghuls climbing up toward the Unicorn on the winged sun, they swung their swords, cutting heads and limbs as they pressed forward. The shock of each impact of his sword made Shono's missing eye throb with delirious pain, but he pressed on. The horses, too, did their part, lashing out with hooves and on occasion teeth, cracking bones and tearing putrid flesh with each blow.

Suddenly, Chagatai loomed before them, roaring his battle cry and sending ghuls sprawling with a sweep of his scimitar. "Cousin!" he cried. "Come, join us! Let us all greet the Lords of Death together!"

"Not today," Shono said, galloping through the gap Chagatai had made him. He held aloft the book. "Unicorn samurai!" he called. "Iuchi Shoan is the key to our salvation. Each moment we buy her is a chance that we all might live. For Shinjo and the Emperor!"

"For Shinjo and the Emperor! For the Lords of Death!" came the call from a dozen Unicorn throats, and Shono was vaulting from Boshi's back, racing to Shoan's side.

"So!" boomed a voice. "I have found the Iuchi sorcerer at last."

"No," Shono breathed. He placed the book in Shoan's outstretched hands and spun around.

Ma'aruf stood ten strides away, within the circle of Unicorn warriors even now fighting against the ghuls. "Your airag awaits you in my mistress's tower," he said. "Now stand aside, that I may kill the sorcerer."

"Never."

"So be it." Ma'aruf folded his arms, nodded his head, and vanished. But Shono was already moving, his watered-steel scimitar glimmering in a flat arc, and when the ifrit appeared behind him, the blade sparked and slid along the stonelike skin of his chest. Shono raised his sword for another strike, and Ma'aruf slapped him with the back of his azure hand. Shono went sprawling while Ma'aruf ran a finger over the chip the sword had cut from his chest. "I don't believe a mortal swordsman has ever cut me before," the djinni said.

Shono pulled himself to his feet, gritting his teeth against the pain of his head and eye and the fresh agony of what must be a broken rib. "Fortune favors the mortal man," he said, and he leapt forward, pure fire, unleashing all his anger and hurling it along the edge of his sword. Ma'aruf lifted one arm to block his blow, as if dismissing a child wielding a willow switch, but the sword sparked again and flaked another chip of the djinni's strange body away.

"Enough of this!" Ma'aruf boomed. "I am commanded to kill the Iuchi sorcerer and any who would stand in my way. I would not harm you, Prince Shono, but you leave me little choice!" He shifted, his bare feet scraping across the stone as he struck: low, low, high.

Earth. Shono read the djinni's style as he danced, like air, away from each strike. *And why not? He has the fortitude of iron and the strength of a mountain.* He blocked one of the djinni's strikes and staggered back, ears ringing and arm aching. *Perhaps literally.*

Shono spared a glance at Shoan. She was hunched over the book with Ryōma, gesturing over a diagram in rust-red ink. *No help there.*

Shono flowed like water, moving with the djinni's next strike and slashing at his legs. *If I can break his stance, I have a chance.* But his sword merely screeched and sparked and left another tiny chip in the djinni's flesh. *Or stone. His stance is so solid he may as well be part of the rock below.* Then Shono blinked. *I have only ever seen his feet planted firmly on stone. He didn't even walk up the stairs with us.*

Then Ma'aruf's fist slammed into his shoulder and sent Shono crashing to his knees. The scimitar skittered away, fallen from numb, nerveless fingers.

"My apologies, sayid," Ma'aruf said, lifting his fist again.

"Spare me," Shono said, and he lashed out with his leg. He surged to his feet, one foot positioned behind Ma'aruf's knee, hip slamming into the djinni, sending Ma'aruf off-balance. The djinni staggered, one foot lifting from the rocky ground, and Shono flowed, water, behind him, blending *ki*, wrapping his arms around the ifrit's chest and *lifting*.

"What!" Ma'aruf bellowed. "Impossible! My strength is of the very earth. You cannot hope to best me in a wrestling match!"

"I believe I just did, sayid," Shono gasped. He held Ma'aruf a finger's breadth above the ground, the djinni kicking and flailing with only ordinary human strength. *And he isn't so heavy as he looks, once you get him off the ground. But I can't do this forever, and if I let even one foot touch the ground he could kill me with a single blow.* "Tell me, my friend. What, precisely, were Mandana's orders to you?"

"'Find and kill every Iuchi sorcerer in the Cradle of the World and the Burning Sands,' she said. 'Let nothing delay you. Kill anyone who would stand in your way.' I have found one, and so I must kill her."

"Shoan-sama!" Shono called.

"Nearly ready, Shono-san," she snapped. "This is slightly more difficult than it looks."

"I'm sorry, Auntie." Shono twisted and hurled Ma'aruf to the ground, as far from Shoan as he could manage. "Iuchi Shoan, I cast you out from the Unicorn Clan. You are *ronin* from this day forth, and no longer may you bear the name Iuchi."

"What?" she gasped. "My lord Shono, please, what—"

"I'm sorry, Auntie," he said again. "Finish your spell or we all die." He turned to Ma'aruf. "Did you catch that, or should I repeat myself in Nehiri?"

"I understood well enough," Ma'aruf said. "Well played, my prince. Mandana will be extremely vexed when I return to her."

"You have the entire Burning Sands to search for any other Iuchi sorcerers that may be lurking there. It seems to me that you should be very, very thorough and take your time before you go anywhere near your mistress again."

Ma'aruf smiled. He folded his arms, bowed his head, and vanished. Shono groaned, found his scimitar, and limped to Shoan's side.

"Auntie," he said.

"I have its name, Shono," Shoan said in a hoarse croak. She looked up from where the book was opened on her knees. Shono's eyes slid away from the crinkled pages, the rust-colored ink, the crawling writing and unsettling illustrations.

"Whose name, Auntie?"

"The demon that binds these ghuls." She stared up at him. Her eyes were red with tears and exhaustion. She trembled. *She's afraid.*

He thought of his father. *"Meishōdō is Name Magic. To know a thing's name is to know its nature, and that knowledge means you can control it."* Daiyu fondled the charm at his throat. *"If you're willing to pay the price."*

"Do it," Shono said.

Shoan nodded and struggled to rise. *She's my mother's age. She looks twenty years older. What troubles her more, me making her rōnin, or that book?* She placed a hand on Ryōma's shoulder and stepped forward. She raised her hands above her head, holding a small piece of rock the same color as the walls below. *A piece of the city itself.* Then she began to sing.

It sounded like the call to prayer, Shono decided, but mournful and foreboding rather than celebratory and humble. But it wavered high above them all, and the ghuls paused as if to listen. When she finished, Shoan cried out in Nehiri, blended with some other language Shono didn't know. "Ho! Go forth! *Tawil at-'Umr! Talmat, talmat!* I release you from this binding, *Qlifot!*"

A great wind tore through the Dead City. The ghuls raised a chorus of hisses, howls, yips, and roars as sand surged in a swirling torrent. When the wind faded, the ghuls were gone; the camp, such as it was, lay in ruins; and a cloud of black-and-red dust danced and twisted in the sky, leaping over the river and settling over al-Zawira.

"No," choked Shoan.

"Good work, sorcerer!" bellowed Chagatai. "You have just saved all our lives."

"But at what cost?" Shono asked.

Shoan pointed a trembling hand at the city, then busied herself with tucking her hair, disordered by the great wind, back behind her ears. A wide white streak ran from her temple to the tips of her previously jet-black locks. *And yet, I do not think that is the price of which she despairs.*

"What happened?" Shono asked again.

"Those creatures, they were all the same demon," Shoan managed after a few deep breaths. "It was bound into service against its will. I set it free." She nodded toward the city. "And now it is taking its vengeance. I fear the city may not survive."

"Let us hope the monster confines its vengeance to Mandana alone," Shono said. "For now, we live, and Mandana and Harun will be in no immediate position to pursue us." He turned to Ryōma. "It's time to snatch a stalemate from the jaws of this defeat."

As the sun came up, Shoan saw to Rashid's wounds—using traditional medicine, ignoring the water talisman of healing at her belt. *Was that her choice, or out of respect for Rashid's Qamarist aversion to sorcery?*

Shono outlined the plan he had half formed when he went looking for Saadiyah. Ryōma listened, nodding, and soon took up the thread, outstripping Shono's explanation. "A pledge of warriors and matériel, mutual defense," he said, clapping his hands and warming to his subject. "Let the deal stand public, and then let the caliph respond. If we give him a chance to back down, then throw in, oh, a three-percent reduction in tariffs and a ceremonial pilgrimage from some Ganzu; he'll be able to save face, and we can prevent any further escalation of the conflict."

Saadiyah snorted. "I wouldn't mind a little escalation, if it ended with his indolent rump off the throne and Mandana's head on a pike."

"What if we want him gone?" Shono asked. "Or what if he refuses?"

"Then it's war, but with the caliph fighting on two fronts while we do the same, it's one that we might actually win." Ryōma shrugged.

Saadiyah took a deep breath and released it, smoothing her now-bloodstained robes. "Let us hope it does not come to that. The Prophet commands peace and brotherhood among all humankind."

Shono fought back a smile. *So, she wars between her desires and the Prophet's Word just as I do with the demands of Bushidō. We are more alike than she thinks.*

Ryōma stood and led them to where Shoan was attending to Rashid in the shadow of one of their few remaining tents. "Shoan-sama," he said. "Sheikh Rashid." He spoke first in Rokugani, then quickly repeated himself in Nehiri. "Between the two of you, we must find a marriage ceremony that will satisfy all parties."

"A what?" Shono asked, following after.

"Of course," Saadiyah said. "That is the traditional way of sealing an alliance in my culture; is it the same in yours?"

"Quite the same nearly everywhere the Unicorn have traveled," Ryōma assured her. He produced paper and a writing kit from somewhere about his person. "Let us discuss the precise terms of the marriage contract—and the alliance. My lord Shono is quite wealthy, of course, and more than willing to pay a generous bride price."

"I won't be a junior wife," Saadiyah said. "I'm his primary wife; I want that down in ink."

"I…have no other wives," Shono said, in a daze.

"That makes it easier," Saadiyah nodded. "I have no other wives, either, at the moment."

Ryōma shoved his hat back and glanced up at Shono's face. "We could have a period of courtship, of course, Shono-sama. Or we could make some other match; perhaps Chagatai, or your sister or brother, or does Lady Saadiyah have any siblings?"

"Two older brothers," Saadiyah said, "but—"

Shono cut her off. "No," he said. "I am not my mother. We will not be spending months on delicate negotiations of this and that point, only to break our word in the end." He turned to where Yumino stood nearby, staring out at the city. "Yumino-san, what is it that you said? Utaku swore no vows, she simply lived her honor?"

"Hai," Yumino said. "Words can get in the way. They can be twisted, interpreted. Actions are where your honor lies."

"I like her," said Saadiyah when Ryōma had finished translating. "So, Shinjo. What is it to be?"

Words were required, sadly, and they spent hours on the terms of the alliance and the contract. It was largely as Ryōma had first proposed, although Saadiyah proved to be a shrewd negotiator in her own right—she would not relent on shipping rights until Shono pointed out that the Unicorn did not control any ports, nor any coastal territory at all. In the end, she insisted on adding them anyway. "Because who knows what might happen in the future?"

The practical upside was that al-Zawira would remain the hub of trade with the East, but Mozedu's merchants would be able to travel as far as Khanbulak. There were details regarding soldiers and matériel to be rendered as aid in the event of war against the Caliphate, and different details against other enemies—including the Lion. *Really a ceremonial contribution for this current war, but that's all we need.*

"Very well," said Ryōma at last. He offered Shono his seal.

Shono took it, feeling its weight in his hand. *If I do this, I've turned my back on Mitsuko entirely.*

"Show some courage, Shinjo," Saadiyah said, perhaps misreading his hesitation. "We could both have it much worse."

Shono thought of Mitsuko. *I could have had it much better, too.* He took a breath and stamped his seal on the paper. "As you say, Saadiyah-san."

"And what now?" Shono asked as he brushed Umeboshi's mane out. Ryōma slouched nearby, letting Patience nose at his sleeves for a treat. *The horses will recover from the terror of last night faster than we will.* "After…the ceremony. Do I ride west, to meet with her father? Or east, to introduce her to my mother?"

"That will be up to you, my lord," said Ryōma. "And I am at your disposal. Chagatai can carry word of what transpired here back to Rokugan as easily as either of us can. And while your mother would sorely desire you to return to the fight against the Lion—"

"Would she, I wonder." Shono rested a hand against Umeboshi's neck, feeling the quiet warmth and solidity of the horse. *Would that I could be so calm.*

"…but if you feel that your attentions are required here, to maintain tranquility, she cannot have any objection." Ryōma bowed to him, shoving Patience away with one hand. "I am happy to draft a letter to both sets of parents, whichever course of action you choose."

"*To maintain tranquility.*" *I could stay in the West for years. Forever, even; securing the alliance with al-Mozedu is as great a benefit as most khans' sons bring their clan. Let Chagatai rule the Unicorn. Don't I deserve to rest?*

He thought of his brother, his sisters. *And how would they fare, in a Rokugan with a Moto Great Khan? Would I never see them again? No. I cannot leave the Unicorn to Chagatai's mercy. He may be a great warrior, but a khan needs to be more than that. We need a khan who knows when to make war and when to make peace—and how to do both.*

He thought of his mother's decision, the choice to plunge them into this war, the one that he had so resented. *An impossible choice. Just as Hama Khutun said, just as Chagatai said.* He whistled Tsubasa out of the herd and brushed him as well.

But at length, it was time. The Unicorn survivors, all twenty of them, gathered outside the Dead City under an ancient olive tree, looking down upon the river. Shoan and Tanaka came to find Shono, to purify him and dress him in his finest clothes.

"This will be the last service I do for you, Shono," Shoan said.

Shono nodded, swallowing the lump in his throat. He wanted to speak to make it right, to restore her to the Unicorn Clan. *But I cannot. What a samurai does, he does with his whole heart. I could not simply pretend to cast her out, not if I expected a djinni like Ma'aruf to accept it as done. And once done, I cannot simply undo it, not without dishonoring both Shoan and myself.* "Auntie," he said.

She brushed his comment aside. "You don't call me that anymore, Shono-sama." She took a deep breath and sighed. "Not the wedding you hoped for, I know. A gaijin bride, and a rōnin priest."

"It doesn't matter," Shono said. "I am ready."

About the Author

Daniel Lovat Clark is a professional nerd. He works as a writer and game developer at Fantasy Flight Games, where his credits include work on Android, Descent: Journeys in the Dark, Arkham Horror, the Legend of the Five Rings Beginner Game, and Legacy of Dragonholt. He lives in the Twin Cities with a dog, a daughter, two cats, and a wife who may technically qualify as the third cat. He learned to ride on Cape Breton Island in Nova Scotia, and got his bachelor's degree in the desert of Arizona, both of which probably had more influence on this book than he would like to admit.

Rokugan

五輪伝

An Empire in Turmoil

A land where honor is stronger than steel. Here, the samurai of the seven Great Clans serve the Emperor as warriors, courtiers, priests, and monks. They live—and die—by the tenets of Bushidō.

The Unicorn Clan gains great wealth and influence from its trade along the Sand Road. Yet, this same foreign contact continues to draw suspicion from the other Great Clans of Rokugan and complicate the Unicorn's place within the Emerald Empire.

Shinjo's Journey

In the years following the Day of Thunder, Shinjo-no-Kami was troubled. She felt that she had failed her fallen brother, Fu Leng, as well as the Empire she had sworn to protect, which had been saved not through the actions of the Kami but through the wisdom of Shinsei and the heroism of seven mortals.

To protect the Empire from any further unknown threats, Shinjo resolved to journey beyond its borders, for how could Rokugan hope to defend itself from dangers about which it knew nothing? And so, she gathered to her the bravest and most faithful of her followers and made preparations to travel to the west. Shinjo released her vassals from their oaths of loyalty before she left on her great journey. Yet many of her people chose to travel with her anyway. The amiable Ide, the wise Iuchi, and the courageous Utaku Shiko (the daughter of Utaku the Thunder) led their followers at Shinjo's side. The Ki-Rin Clan had not even left Rokugan yet, and already they had changed and become something different from all the clans they would leave behind.

In the year 45 by Isawa reckoning, Shinjo and the Ki-Rin passed beyond the border of Rokugan and outside of all knowledge of the Emerald Empire. They carried with them a mirror, crafted by Isawa and blessed by Hantei-no-Kami, said to reflect the image of its twin so that Shinjo could continue to speak with her brothers and sisters in the Empire. They also bore a sandalwood fan, a gift from Doji-no-Kami to her favored sister.

The Ujik and the Moto

The Ki-Rin's journey almost ended in disaster scarcely one-hundred *li* beyond their own borders, when they found themselves wandering the desolate and punishing Plain of Wind and Stone. This desert was brutally cold in winter and perishingly hot in summer, with so little water and food that the Ki-Rin began to starve. To make matters worse, they were soon attacked by a band of horseback-riding nomads known as Ujik. Although the courage and skill of Shinjo's samurai were second to none, doing battle with such a mobile and flexible enemy seemed impossible until Shinjo and Utaku Shiko captured a handful of Ujik horses and adopted Ujik tactics.

Impressed by the prowess of Shinjo's people, the Ujik halted their raids and began to trade in peace with Ide and the rest of the clan. With the addition of Ujik horses and by adopting Ujik nomadic practices and herding techniques, the Ki-Rin soon were no longer starving, but began to thrive. In time, many of the Ujik joined the clan, binding themselves through promises of fellowship and a number of strategic marriages. These Ujik, now called the Moto, soon became a vital part of the Ki-Rin Clan, and the friendship of the Ki-Rin allowed the Ujik to press back against their traditional enemies, human and otherwise, at the limits of their territory.

The Ki-Rin spent "a generation," perhaps as much as one hundred years, living among the Ujik. By the time they were ready to move on, every single Ki-Rin was mounted atop a sturdy Ujik desert horse, and the entire clan had adopted the Ujik saddle and, even more importantly, the stirrup. Now, when they made war, Shinjo's people fought from horseback.

Shinjo's Captivity

During their conflict with the Ujik, Ki-Rin scouts and explorers had been hard at work probing the limits of the unassailable mountains to the south and the trackless deserts to the west, the so-called Burning Sands. In time, the Ki-Rin Clan saw no other course, and rode west once more.

Traveling across the Burning Sands was the greatest challenge yet faced by the Ki-Rin, but when they reached the lush river valleys of the Cradle of the World, they were rewarded with splendor and gifts such as they could scarcely believe. The pharaohs of Rempet claimed divine lineage from the Sun God, Shem, and they declared Shinjo-no-Kami to be their sister from afar. She and her followers were lavished with riches by the sorcerer-king Nephrentep. Half-dead with hunger and thirst, the Ki-Rin eagerly accepted the hospitality of Rempet, even as Shinjo and some of the elders of the clan were troubled that the priests and nobles of the city openly practiced slavery.

Nephrentep's hospitality was a ruse. As soon as the Ki-Rin let down their guard, the pharaoh struck, snatching Shinjo from among them and spiriting her away to his temple-palace. The sorcerer-king's undying guard attacked the Ki-Rin and drove them into hiding. Iuchi declared that the sinister priests of Rempet were blood sorcerers and that they intended to use Shinjo-no-Kami's divine blood in a ritual to prolong Nephrentep's life. The Ki-Rin all agreed that they would die before they allowed such a fate to befall their beloved Shinjo.

Clever Ide found allies in Rempet: the al-Qamari, a secret organization devoted to opposing the Sun Kings. Together, the Ki-Rin and the al-Qamari staged a daring attack on Nephrentep's temple-palace. The attack seemed doomed to failure, as the pharaoh's magic and his undying guard were too strong for the rescuers, until the gods themselves intervened: the moon blotted out the sun, throwing day into night. The moon ruled supreme until the wicked king was cast down and Shinjo was liberated. Once freed, Shinjo united the Ki-Rin Clan and the oppressed peoples of Rempet to destroy the corrupt empire of the sorcerer-kings.

A Journey out of Knowledge

Not long after destroying the Empire of Rempet, Shinjo gathered her clan to her and pronounced that they would go their separate ways. "The world is too big," she said, "for those on any one journey to ever discover it all." She divided the Ki-Rin Clan into five hordes and sent them each in a different direction. Shinjo took her Blue Horde west. Iuchi took his Green Horde south. Moto Chabi Khan took her White Horde north, continuing the journey across the Burning Sands. Utaku Shiko took her Purple Horde east, into the Ivory Kingdoms. And Ide's Golden Horde remained in place, exploring the coast of the Conqueror's Sea.

The accounts brought back by the three hordes returning to Rokugan—now calling themselves the Unicorn Clan—are sometimes unbelievable. They told of empires of snake-like beings, raiders with the body of a horse and the torso of a human, giants with only one eye, cursed pits and blessed valleys, and the Unicorn itself, a horselike spirit of water and fire that some say fathered Shinjo's children. Tragically, Iuchi's Green Horde never returned. According to rumor, they still ride the world, seeking its uttermost limits.

The Ride through Shadow

At length, the time came to return to Rokugan. Rather than cross the Burning Sands, the Unicorn rode south of the Pillar of the Sky mountains, into the tangled forests and steep valleys of the Ivory Kingdoms. Although now mounted on the finest horses in the world, the Unicorn struggled to make good time, as they were frequently turned back by the people and creatures they encountered among the hills and valleys. When they reached the eastern edge of the Ivory Kingdoms, they found one more barrier in their path: the twisted, unnatural forest of the western Shadowlands.

According to the Ide chroniclers, it took the Unicorn Clan forty years to cross from the Conqueror's Sea to the Kaiu Wall in Rokugan. It seems an improbable duration for a journey that can now be made along the Sand Road in a handful of months, but the modern route does not account for the Shadowlands. In that cursed place, life and death, and even time itself, do not have the same meaning they do in the rest of the world. Who can say how long the Unicorn rode and fought their way through those blighted lands? Surely, they proceeded with the same mix of boldness and caution that had guided them across the Burning Sands, stopping in places of relative safety and sending forth their scouts, before plunging headlong into danger. The Ide Chronicles are difficult to reconcile with the Imperial Histories in this period.

In 815 IC, the Unicorn finally escaped the Shadowlands. Judged to be an invading Tainted horde by the Crab, they used their foreign magics to smash a hole in the Kaiu Wall and enter Rokugan near Razor of the Dawn Castle. They rode through the Shinomen Forest, up the River of Gold, and across the Spine of the World Mountains, evading or overrunning anyone who opposed them. Finally, they reached their ancestral homeland—and the enormous Lion Clan army that had claimed it for their own. To every samurai they met upon their return to Rokugan, the Unicorn were nothing more than barbarian invaders.

Fortunately for the Unicorn (and the Lion), Ide emissaries brought Doji-no-Kami's sandalwood fan with them to the court of the Crane and thereby proved their clan were the children of Shinjo returned. The Emperor, at the Crane's request, granted the Unicorn claim to their ancestral lands and ended the war. After nearly eight hundred years of exile, the Unicorn were finally home.

The Cradle of the World

Surrounded by deserts to the east and west and seas to the north and south, the "land between two rivers" has been a flowering garden of civilization since the dawn of time. The residents of this fertile region have long maintained that it was in this land that civilization first arose, and so they call their homeland the Cradle of the World.

OLD REMPET

From the east, where Lord Sun rises in the morning, came a mortal woman in the final days of her pregnancy. She was soon delivered of a divine child, the son of Shem, the Sun God, whom she named Horiz-Rem. This child rose to become the first pharaoh priest-king of Rempet, the Kingdom of the Sun God. Horiz-Rem had many wives, lived a supernaturally long life, and fathered more than ninety children, who became the ruling nobility of Rempet. Within a handful of mortal lifetimes, Rempet became the greatest empire in the world, and until its fall, its pharaohs all traced their lineage back to Horiz-Rem, and through him to Shem himself.

Thanks to their divine blood, the noble priest-kings of Rempet took as a given their right to rule over all of humanity. As these rulers were sorcerers, there was little the people of the Cradle or its neighboring tribes could do to stop them. Even the djinn were helpless before the pharaohs. Rempet soon enslaved entire tribes, using them to grow crops and build enormous pyramidal temples and tombs. Only the al-Qamari opposed the pharaohs, but these "Children of the Moon" were forced to operate at night, striking from hiding, and were seldom more than a nuisance.

However, with each successive generation, the divine essence of Horiz-Rem was spread more and more thinly. The pharaohs, unwilling to accept a lifespan of a mere century or two, began to delve deep into their sorcerous arts for means to prolong their lives. Through the use of blood magic, they defied death, replacing some of their slaves with undying servants. It is believed the rulers of Old Rempet were the first to discover the secret of unliving life.

When Shinjo, herself a divine being, came to Rempet, the pharaoh Nephrentep immediately seized on a plan to use her blood in a sorcerous ritual to bestow upon himself the divinity of Horiz-Rem. The scheme ended in disaster, however. An alliance of Shinjo's followers and revolutionaries from within the enslaved Nehiri tribes stormed the seat of Nephrentep's power, slew him, and ended the reign of the pharaohs.

THE NAMELESS PROPHET

Over the century that followed, Rempet died by pieces. One by one, various external threats and slave revolts led by the al-Qamari toppled the sorcerer-priests from their thrones. The Cradle of the World collapsed into warring tribes and city-states, where djinn haunted the wild places and rogue sorcerers stalked the shadows.

Into this chaotic scene came the Nameless Prophet. Some claim he was born into a pre-Rempet Nehiri noble house, others that he was the son of a slave and a pharaoh, still others that he was a traveler from a distant land. In any case, the Prophet brought new teachings and a new way of life to the Cradle of the World, and these did much to bring peace to the region. He claimed to bring the Word of Heaven to both humans and djinn, and that service to Heaven and not earthly power was the true path forward for humankind. His first followers took on the mantle of the al-Qamari, and the new faith became known as Qamarism.

The Prophet (his name has been concealed for fear of sorcerers wielding Name Magic) founded a new empire in what is now the City of God in the Mountains of Shem. He led his followers down into the valley of the Queen's River, converting the Nehiri tribes and city-states he found there by prayer or by strength of arms, as required. Soon, Qamarism had spread across the entire land between the two rivers, and throughout the Mountains of Shem and the Mountains of Qamar.

THE PROPHET'S END

At length, the Prophet's time came to an end. Although some hold that the Nameless Prophet simply moved on to bring his teachings to the rest of the world, most scholars agree that he died and was buried in the City of God, at an advanced age, and after fathering many children. The Prophet's death left his nascent empire without a ruler, so his followers gathered together to decide who should lead them. Eventually, they chose from within their number a single great and wise thinker, who became the first caliph, and so the Qamari Caliphate was created.

THE SABORIM

The Qamarist faith has suffered many schisms throughout its history. The first dates from the death (or disappearance) of the Prophet, when a key sect of his followers refused to accept the authority of the caliph chosen to succeed him. The Saborim ("those who wait") have long had a strained relationship with mainstream Qamarism. Still, their dedication to the Word of the Prophet and their scholarship and skill in medicine and alchemy are widely admired, so Saborim communities are generally tolerated throughout the Caliphate.

The Spread of the Word

The first caliph, Mahmoud ibn Mansur, immediately founded a new capital for his Caliphate in a prime location on the King's River. Al-Zawira, also known as the Round City, soon became the jewel in the Caliphate's crown and the envy of all other cities in the world. But Mahmoud did not rest there.

By Sword and by Book

The Qamari Caliphate began in the heart of the Nehiri homeland, between the two rivers, but it soon spread far across the Cradle of the World. The Caliphate first turned its attention to the Twilight Kings, the undying remnants of Old Rempet who lived out cruel pantomimes of their living days even as the desert sands swallowed their once-verdant cities whole. Bolstered by their faith and with the aid of the Twilight Kings' remaining living slaves, the Caliphate cast down the mummified pharaohs and united the last of the Nehiri tribes. In the North, the warlike Suhili fought a desperate battle against the monstrous legions of the baleful god Zeth, who ages earlier had drowned in the Cursed Sea after doing battle with Shem. The Caliphate came to their aid, and the Suhili accepted both the Word of the Prophet and the leadership of the caliph.

The Sogdan city-states in the West were plagued by internecine war and the depredations of a terrible manticore, whose trickery and treachery created fresh conflict whenever peace emerged. Emissaries from the Caliphate brought a message of peace and fellowship to the Sogdans, and clever Qamarist teachers bested the manticore at its riddle game, breaking its influence on the region. Even the proud Bandar across the Sea of Jewels, who had resisted the early imperial ambitions of both Mweneta in the far south and the Caliphate, eventually bowed to the teachings of the Prophet, and their leaders became emirs under the caliph's authority.

The Lands and Tribes of the Caliphate

The heartland of the Caliphate encompasses the traditional homeland of the sun-browned Nehiri, the black-haired people of the river. Consisting of the valley between the King's River and the Queen's River, the so-called Cradle of the World is the most fertile land in all the Caliphate, lush with gardens, orchards, and bountiful crops. The Nehiri who live there are firm in their faith and devoted to scholarship and learning—indeed, their capital, al-Zawira, is known by another name, the "City of Books."

Across the Mountains of Shem to the west lie the city-states of the Sogdans. Renowned as builders and engineers, the olive-skinned Sogdans build great towers and ziggurats. Their grandest city-state, Ninua, boasts a great ziggurat standing proud on the coast of the Conqueror's Sea; its beacon can be seen from a great distance to aid sailors and pilgrims on their journeys. In ancient days, so the legend goes, the Sogdan people were all united and worked together to build a tower tall enough to reach the Heavens. But the gods—or God, according to the new Qamarist understanding of the world—became angry at the Sogdans' pride, struck down their tower, and cursed them to live in strife with one another forever more. Since then, the city-states of the Sogdans have often gone to war with one another, and even in this time of relative peace and prosperity, the Sogdans have a gloomy outlook, blaming every misfortune on their ancestral curse.

The Cursed Sea, home of the drowned god Zeth, lies to the north, and the steppes that run up to its shores are the home of the Suhili, the people of the plain. The fair-skinned Suhili still live a seminomadic life, as many tribes did in the days before Rempet. They have only one great city, Zymarkin, the City of the Bronze Gate. Proud warriors, the Suhili fight an eternal battle against the dragons, monsters, and minions of Zeth that emerge from the Cursed Sea whenever the moon is dark. Suhili prefer to fight from horseback or from their swift and deadly chariots whenever possible, and they have long since adopted the stirrup from their contact with the Ki-Rin Clan.

The dark-skinned Bandar live to the west, across the Sea of Jewels. Divided roughly between the nomadic shepherds of the highlands and the city dwellers along the seacoast and the north-flowing Serpent River, the Bandar are in fact a dozen or more allied and related peoples united by a shared language and a long history of intermarriage. These close alliances have turned the Bandar into a mighty merchant kingdom, controlling trade between the rest of the Caliphate to the east, the Mweneta Empire to the south, and the Vyzantari Kingdom across the Conqueror's Sea. The various Bandar emirates, especially the city of Mozedu, are among the most powerful and wealthy of any in the Qamari Caliphate.

The Sand Road

When the Unicorn Clan returned to Rokugan in 815 IC, they found a land as foreign to them as any in which they had ever traveled. Despite their best efforts, the Unicorn struggled to be accepted by their cousins in the Emerald Empire, and Shinjo's people lived always in a state of conflict with the other clans. Weakened by their long ride through the Shadowlands and still struggling to adapt to a new way of life, the Unicorn made a number of missteps in the first few decades after their return that not only limited their influence and respect among the other clans, but threatened their very existence. In short, the other clans were wealthier and more respected than the Unicorn, and almost all were more numerous. Aside from their horses, which the Unicorn were reluctant to part with, they had little to offer the Emperor or the other clans.

In 845 IC, a new Great Khan assumed the leadership of the Unicorn Clan. Shinjo Temujin resolved to find a new source of wealth and power for his clan, and so he ordered one hundred of his finest scouts to search for a safe route through the Burning Sands to the Cradle of the World and the Ivory Kingdoms. The exotic artifacts and treasures of the West, Temujin reasoned, would give the Unicorn long sought-after leverage in their negotiations with the other clans and might finally earn the Unicorn the respect they deserved. By 850 IC, after the death of nearly half of Temujin's scouts, a route was finally established, and the Sand Road was born.

Trade with the West soon made the Unicorn one of the richest clans in the Empire. The silk, tea, and art they sent west were repaid with caravans bursting with nephrite jade, precious stones and metals, honey, sugar, opium, cotton, and gaijin artifacts of all descriptions. The Unicorn also eagerly traded horses and other livestock in both directions, but these riches they kept to themselves. The other imports they sold on to the clans and Imperial families. This made them an invaluable part of Rokugan's economy and gave them the time and allies required for them to grow and recover from their long exile. In time, the city of Khanbulak on the border of the Empire became the largest and richest city in all of the Unicorn lands—and the Moto family, which controls it, grows ever more powerful, despite their great losses upon their return to Rokugan.

THE WAY STATIONS

Shinjo Temujin ordered that a way station be built every fifty li (about a half day's walk on foot) along the entire length of the Sand Road. These way stations were to be equipped with storehouses, paddocks for horses and camels, and cisterns or wells for water, and they were to be guarded and resupplied when necessary by the khan's own soldiers. While the reality of this order has never quite been realized, as many way stations are still unfinished or undersupplied, enough of the Sand Road is so provisioned as to make a journey across its length merely difficult rather than punishing and probably fatal. Gaijin merchants who make use of the Sand Road must pay sizable tariffs to contribute to its upkeep, but they usually judge the cost reasonable considering the benefits the way stations offer. Thus, the system remains in place and may even one day be finished.

GEOGRAPHY

According to the most recent survey, conducted during the reign of Shinjo Khulan Khan, the Sand Road runs some 12,500 li from Khanbulak to al-Zawira. A message-rider changing horses at each way station can make the entire journey in just over two weeks, but most caravans take something closer to four months.

From Khanbulak, the Sand Road twists down through a rocky landscape and into the highlands of the Plain of Wind and Stone. Dry and windswept, cold in the winter and hot in the summer, the Plain of Wind and Stone is home to the nomadic Ujik; herds of horses, deer, and camels; zilants; yaryonds; death worms; and very little else. The Moto family of the Unicorn Clan maintains close ties with its Ujik cousins. These relations are generally good, although it's never wise to discount the threat of rebellious or desperate Ujik who turn to banditry or agitate for war.

To the south and west of the Plain of Wind and Stone, the Sand Road climbs into the lower foothills of the Pillar of the Sky. These mountains, it is said, are the tallest in the world, and the people, trolls, and goblins who live there are tough and often violent. Strangely, some of the Tegensai tribes that live there practice a tradition that seems to have its roots in Shinseism, and some Unicorn shugenja make regular visits to the few temples that cling to the upper slopes. As for the rest of the Unicorn Clan, they trade for the furs and dogs the Tegensai offer when they can and fight off Tegensai bandits when they must.

Beyond the Pillar of the Sky, the Sand Road descends to the seemingly endless, scorched plain of the Burning Sands proper, which extend to the banks of the King's River in the Cradle of the World. Often shunned as an empty wasteland, the Burning Sands is actually quite varied in character and climate, and during its brief rainy season, large parts of the desert bloom with frantic, beautiful life. But for the rest of the year, the Burning Sands are some of the most desolate and impossible terrain in the world, full of dust storms and scorching heat, and offering neither food nor water to speak of. The only human life is a few scattered nomadic tribes and oasis cities, among them canyon-shadowed Emshaal and Ürumzi on the Dead Lake.

The most important of these oases is the Hidden Valley, almost precisely halfway between Khanbulak and al-Zawira. It is home to the Ganzu people, loyal vassals of the Khan of Khans for a century. The Green River flows down from the Pillar of the Sky and carves a narrow valley from the sandstone hills of the Burning Sands, eventually drying out into a mucky wash of sun-scorched clay, never reaching any lake or sea. But in that valley lie fertile farms and orchards and a small city of the Ganzu. For protection from the heat, the Ganzu build their homes half beneath the ground, and for defense from enemies, they keep even the spires of their temple below the level of the canyon walls; as a result, the farms, the river, and the city are all quite secret. The Hidden Valley is invisible from more than a dozen paces away in any direction. Who knows how many roving bands of foes have passed by, never the wiser?

Djinn and Sorcery

When the Ki-Rin first crossed the Burning Sands, they were dismayed to discover that their prayers to the kami went unanswered: there were no kami here. Instead, they soon discovered that beings of smokeless fire, called djinn, dwelled in the hidden and remote regions. Entirely new prayers, offerings, and rites would be required to commune with them, and Iuchi looked to the local people to learn how to do so.

NAME MAGIC

In addition to a type of blood sorcery almost indistinguishable from the *mahō* of Rokugan, the sorcerers of Rempet had practiced a form of Name Magic. By speaking the True Name of a djinni, demon, or other supernatural being, a sorcerer could compel the spirit into service or bind it to an object such as a lamp or ring. Some powerful sorcerers could use their Name Magic on mortals. Qamarists refuse to speak the name of the Prophet or of their God for fear of being accused of sorcery.

MANTICORES

Also known as sphinxes, manticores are terrible and powerful monsters who have been the bane of civilizations since time immemorial. Manticores are known to take human form when they desire, but their true forms resemble great hunting cats or birds of prey—or sometimes both together—with human faces. They eat only human flesh and are said to take great delight in secrets, riddles, and wordplay. Their magic is as powerful as that of any human sorcerer, and some sorcerers seek them out to learn their mystic arts.

Due to the Prophet's disapproval of slavery, sorcery is generally banned throughout the Caliphate. Nevertheless, many caliphs and emirs have kept court sorcerers in their employ. These positions are justified by the argument that as long as the sorcerers are negotiating fair trades with the spirits, no forbidden slavery is occurring. Still, some courts have outright ignored the Prophet's prohibitions.

COURTS OF DJINN

The djinn belong to this world, not Heaven or Hell, and are an older race than humankind. There are many tribes and nations of djinn, and their numbers are impossible to calculate. Djinn may nonetheless be helpfully divided into several distinct types, three of which are described below:

Jann, the weakest djinn, are flighty, ephemeral creatures of smokeless fire. They are often invisible, and while possessed of myriad powers no mortal can hope to equal, they are simple, strange, and fey beings, relatively easy to appease and even control. Jann are the most numerous of the djinn and the type most frequently bound by Name Magic.

Ifrits are often possessed of physical bodies, which may be replete with animalistic features such as horns or the snouts of jackals. Their physical prowess is formidable, and many are able to fly great distances in the blink of an eye, lift entire palaces above their heads, or perform other incredible feats at the whims of their masters. More human than jann, ifrits are proud beings who are prone to flattery and sometimes reward humble or pious humans. Like all djinn, they can and do vanish in an instant.

The *marids* are the greatest of the djinn, combining all the physical power of the ifrits with all the mystical abilities of the jann. Marids, when they choose to manifest a body, often appear very humanlike, but of enormous size and noble bearing. Marids were once worshipped as gods by primitive and superstitious humans. Only the most powerful or foolhardy sorcerers would attempt to bind a marid with Name Magic, as these proud beings will surely take a most painful revenge should they ever break free.

The Secret History of the Unicorn

This document, maintained by Ide chroniclers during the entire length of the Unicorn's exodus from Rokugan, was begun by Ide himself. It is the only written record of that time to survive to the present day, but it has never been shared with the rest of Rokugan, for fear that it will be used as evidence against the clan in the Imperial Court.

Many of the stories contained in the *Secret History* are, by necessity, secondhand or apocryphal, as the chronicle was maintained only by the Golden Horde during the time the clan was divided. Several of its stories about the other hordes seem fanciful or supernatural, but according to the Ide, this is no reason to discount them as false.

SHINJO AND THE UNICORN

Shinjo-no-Kami's party was sorely distressed, lacking food and water after its journey across the Black Plain. At length, the travelers found a green grove centered on a pool of clean water, and their spirits were lifted. But Shinjo warned them: "Eat nothing, harm no animal, and drink no water. This is the spirits' place, and I must ask them for their blessing lest we anger them."

And so Shinjo went into that place, and her people made camp and awaited her return. After eight days, Utaku Chiaki, desperate to feed her people, took up her bow and shot a deer, then took her waterskin and gathered water from the grove. The people ate and drank and were grateful, but suddenly the grove vanished, the pool of water turned murky and foul, and no trace was left of the plenty of the oasis. And there was no sign of Shinjo. Then, a brilliant horned horse of white light appeared and galloped to the west, and so the people followed it, and soon they found the green grove again, and a pool of water even more beautiful and clean than the last. They waited there for Shinjo, and after eight more days, she appeared to them.

"The Unicorn spirit of this place is wroth," she said, "for the life of the deer you slew. Only another life can appease him."

"But lady!" cried her followers, misunderstanding her words. "We will be lost without you!"

"Fear not," she said. "I will not die, and you may stay here a time and eat and drink to your heart's content, for the Unicorn has given us his blessing." And the people saw then that she was with child, and so they made their home in the green grove for some months, until Shinjo was at last delivered of five beautiful children. "One of these children must return here to dwell with the Unicorn and to replace the life you took," she said. "But I will not make that choice for them. In time, they will be old enough to decide for themselves."

Shinjo and the World-Devourer

Shinjo-no-Kami stood on the shore of the Endless Sea, and she knew that she could go no further, for no lands lay ahead. A great shape rose in the water, like a serpent or a demon that towered above the tallest tree. "Turn back, little god," spoke the monster, "for I am the mother of earth and sea, and I hunger."

Shinjo named the being Orochi, the Great Serpent. "And what appeases your hunger?" Shinjo asked, for her compassion for all things stayed her hand.

"All that lives, all that breathes, the very soil and the earth itself, I will consume until all the world is gone, and only then will I birth a new world to consume," said the monster. And Shinjo saw that here was the great enemy beyond the borders of Rokugan that she had rode out to find.

"Go back," she said to her followers. "Return to the Emerald Empire, that none of you remember, and make it your home, for they will need your wisdom and your strength in the time to come." And she drew her sword, and mounted her steed as swift as the air, and rode out above the waves to do battle with the world-devourer. Once, twice, three times she rode in a circle around the beast, slashing with her sword, and on the fourth pass the creature opened wide its jaws and swallowed half the ocean, and Shinjo along with it, and together they vanished beneath the waves.

But they say that Shinjo lived on past that day, for the belly of such a great beast contains all the world that it has already swallowed, and perhaps Shinjo has already killed the beast and rides even now to return to her people. After all, her promise was: "I will always return."